THE VERY DANGEROUS SISTERS
OF INDIGO MCCLOUD

The VERY DANGEROUS SISTERS of INDIGO McCLOUD

JOHN HEARNE

THE VERY DANGEROUS SISTERS OF INDIGO MCCLOUD

First published in 2021 by
Little Island Books
7 Kenilworth Park
Dublin 6W
Ireland

First published in the USA by Little Island in 2023

ISBN: 978-1-912417-76-6

Cover design by Ailsa Cullen
Cover illustration © Flavia Sorrentino, 2021, licensed exclusively
by THe Bright Agency: www.thebrightagency.com
Typeset and design by Nolan Book Design
Copyedited and proofread by Emma Dunne

Printed in Poland by Drukarnia Skleniarz

Little Island receives FInancial support from
the Arts Council / An Chomhairle Ealaíon

10 9 8 7 6 5 4 3 2

For my mother, Mary, who lit the spark
and my wife, Marie, who keeps it alive

1

The Unfortunate Fate
of Lucy Jones

Indigo McCloud stood by an open window and stared out at the damp, grubby cobbles of Adenoid Terrace.

It was getting dark. Smoke from the twin smokestacks of the plastic Christmas-tree factory was settling gently on the street outside, covering it and everything else in the little town of Blunt in grey–black grime.

Through the still, smoky air, Indigo could hear the strains of a new batch of accordions being tested in the nearby factory mingling with the braying of the donkeys in the very large donkey sanctuary on the edge of town.

Indigo McCloud was a skilled watcher. He could sit perfectly still for hours in the unlikeliest of places: the roof of his school on Beetroot Street or the top of the Crappy Tower – the town's most prominent landmark. He particularly liked the campanile of the Cathedral of St Dolores of the Unending Sorrows and the radio antenna on the roof of the tweezers factory. In these and many other high places – Blunt had no shortage of tall and ponderous buildings – Indigo would watch the cars creep along the streets and the tiny figures on the pavements far below, or follow the course of the River Blunt as it arced about the Eelfields on the edge of town. He would watch with perfect calm, still as a gargoyle, safe in the knowledge that nothing of any significance ever happened in Blunt.

Now, however, something of significance was about to happen. He could taste it on his tongue and feel it in the tips of his fingers. As a result, Indigo McCloud could not sit still.

'What time is it?' he asked.

'Five fifty-eight,' said Polly without looking up from her work.

Her desk was strewn with bits of wire and metal and she was holding a soldering iron like a pencil over a small plastic something. There was the quietest hiss as the solder melted, then cooled, at the junction of two wires. Everything in her bedroom – the bedspread, the computer, the desk on which it sat, the walls, the ceiling, the window frames, the curtain, the two chairs, the soldering iron and the wires at which she worked – was a shade of brown called burnt umber. It was a colour that Polly found especially calming.

'Fifteen seconds, right?' said Indigo, pushing his fingers through his hair, which was almost completely grey. 'It'll take her fifteen seconds to cross the street. What can happen in fifteen seconds?'

'My calculations,' said Polly, 'suggest that it will take Lucy Jones between 11.94 and 23.82 seconds to cross from her home at Number 37 to her weekly mandolin lesson with Monsieur Brunel at Number 46. The range is dependent on a wide variety of factors, including but not restricted to the pace at which Lucy walks, the presence of pigeons or other birds in the street at the time, the possibility of a –'

'What have pigeons to do with anything?'

'Lucy has a bird phobia. If there is a bird in her path on the way to Monsieur Brunel's, she will take a detour around it.'

'How do you know she has a bird phobia?'

Polly turned to her computer. Her fingers danced on the keyboard. 'It would appear to stem from an incident when she was three years old, in which she accidently locked herself into a Škoda Octavia with a neighbour's parakeet. The bird's name was Billy Feathers.'

'How –?'

'And on her eighth birthday, her Auntie Ann gave her a stuffed owl. When she tore the paper from the present and saw that it was a bird, she went into catatonic shock and did not come round for three hours.'

'Polly. How do you know all this?'

Polly looked up. Her face was dominated by a pair of large-framed glasses. Her long black hair was parted exactly down the middle and gathered into two tight pigtails of equal length.

'I cross-referenced medical records with police incident reports from the national database, then performed a series of statistical regressions which isolated –'

Indigo held up his hands. 'OK, great, that's great, thank you, Polly.' He pointed to the device on her desk. 'Are you finished with that?'

She extended the apparatus and showed Indigo how to hook it over his right ear.

'It has a range of up to 5.62 kilometres,' she said, 'and therefore should allow us to remain in contact within the limits of the town.'

They tested the headset and, once reassured that it was working, Indigo turned and resumed his silent vigil by the window.

Adenoid Terrace consisted of two rows of tightly huddled red-brick houses, each one more or less identical to the one beside it. These rows faced each other across a cobbled road pocked with potholes. Most of the houses were in quite a bad state of repair, with crumbling bricks, leaky roofs and the odd broken window patched with cardboard. One, Number 18, was completely boarded up.

Indigo now divided his gaze between Lucy's door and the door of his own house, Number 21, which was also visible a little further along the street.

Meanwhile, not far away, the significant event which Indigo had been anticipating began to unfold. Up on the top of Snook Hill stood a little playground surrounded by a temporary security fence. This had been erected by a team of demolition experts earlier in the day. The playground was to be blown up in order to widen the road to make way for the enormous trucks which transported the plastic Christmas trees from Blunt to every other part of the country. It was now just after six o'clock. The demolition team had left for the evening. The site should have been deserted but it wasn't.

If you listened carefully you could hear clicking noises from the large yellow digger that stood in a corner of the site. There was a sudden fizz of electricity and the engine roared to life. The person in the cab now pulled a cushion from the backpack she carried and placed it on the seat. She then climbed up, peered over the large steering wheel, checked her watch and placed her left hand on the gear stick. This hand was clad in a thin woollen glove, the little finger of which was empty and tied in a knot. The gear stick moved easily into first and the digger edged slowly across the doomed playground, past the *No Trespassing* signs, through a gap in the fence and out onto the road that led down Snook Hill towards Adenoid Terrace.

Now it began to gather speed.

'Four minutes past six,' said Indigo McCloud, staring at Lucy's dull green door. 'Any second now.'

Lionel Piper, the glue man, sold glue door to door from the little trolley he pushed about the streets of Blunt. He was steering his trolley across the road at the foot of Snook Hill when a large yellow digger, travelling at three times the speed limit, came barrelling towards him. He dived out of the way just in time as the digger smashed into the trolley, destroying it completely.

Now the door of Number 37 opened and Lucy Jones, a bright-eyed girl of around Indigo's age, emerged. She had short spiky hair, and she carried a mandolin case in one hand and a folder of sheet music in the other.

Indigo, his body tense as a piano string, stared hard at Lucy, whose expression betrayed no hint of anxiety.

'Hurry up, Lucy,' he muttered.

'You are stressed,' said Polly. 'Would you like me to talk about ducks?'

'Not now, Polly. Hang on. Can you hear that?'

At this moment, the digger, completely covered in glue, roared around the corner, lowering its bucket as it came. Lucy turned to see the monstrous thing bearing down upon her. Before she could even gather her resources to scream, she had been scooped up in the glue-filled bucket and whisked off down the street. Scattered sheets of music fluttered gently to the ground in the wake of the digger.

Quick as a flash, Indigo leaped out onto the sill, grabbed the gutter and flipped effortlessly onto the roof. He scampered to the top just in time to see the digger turn right onto Brain Street. He squinted into the smoke but he could not make out the identity of the person at the wheel.

As the digger accelerated away from him, Indigo sprinted along the rooftops to the end of the terrace, slid down the tiles and leaped onto the high wall that adjoined the neighbouring Brain Street Flats. He skipped across the top of the wall and climbed the brickwork like a spider, reaching the top of the four-storey building in seconds. From there, he could see the digger weave in and out of the traffic, swerve onto the wrong side of the road, then mount the pavement. Cars collided in its wake; pedestrians dived out of the way.

'Where are they taking her?'

'I don't know, Indigo.' Polly's voice crackled over the headset and Indigo started. He had forgotten he was still wearing it.

'They can't be going far. The further they take her, the greater the risk of getting caught. Quick, Polly, give me a list of places within a two-kilometre radius of Brain Street. Not houses, nothing residential.'

Indigo heard Polly's fingers on the keyboard. 'Blunt Darts Palace at Number 53.'

'They've already passed that.'

'The shoe-stretching plant, the old prison, the new prison and the breadcrumb factory.'

The digger showed no signs of slowing down. Anything which got in its way was either blasted to one side or crushed beneath its wheels. From where he stood, Indigo watched the digger charge past all of the places Polly had listed – or at least almost all.

'The breadcrumb factory,' said Indigo, 'right at the end of Brain Street. Must be!'

He dashed to the edge of the roof, flipped over and landed like a cat on the balcony below. He then moved rapidly from balcony to balcony, hit the pavement and took off down the street. He did not notice the large formations of geese flying high above the town, but he did see, as he wove through the pedestrians that crowded the pavement, the yellow digger smash through the gates of the breadcrumb factory.

Since it was past six, the factory was almost entirely deserted. The digger careered across the yard, then came to a sudden, shrieking stop before a row of large steel containers ranged beside the perimeter wall. Lucy Jones, despite being completely covered in glue, remained largely unhurt as she was catapulted out of the bucket of the digger and into breadcrumb hopper Number 4. Mercifully, this large steel container was half-full of breadcrumbs and these broke her fall. Quivering with shock, she dragged herself from the hopper and, still clutching her mandolin case, she staggered out into the factory yard. She was now completely covered in glue-stuck breadcrumbs.

Blunt lies directly in the migration path of the white-fronted Greenland goose, which flies over the town in large numbers every spring on its way to its summer feeding grounds. Just as Lucy made it to the yard, the flock of geese looked down and saw a curious figure stumbling about, apparently composed of breadcrumbs. It was an exceptionally tempting sight for a goose nearing the end of a long journey, and all four hundred and thirty-seven of them swooped down and attacked Lucy.

The first people on the scene were two Chinese tourists, who had mistakenly disembarked from their tour bus, thinking they had arrived in Cragmire, a quaint little town ten miles further down the road, famed for its cow museum. They had been puzzling over a map outside the breadcrumb factory gates and had to scramble out of the way when the digger came rushing towards them. Things happened so quickly that by the time they picked themselves up and peered in through the mangled gates, the geese had descended and Lucy was invisible beneath a livid mass of flapping wings and stabbing beaks. The digger had been abandoned. It stood, just where it had braked moments before, one door open, the cab empty. These tourists were never subsequently interviewed by the police, but if they had been, they would have said that they glimpsed a slight figure dressed in blue disappearing over the wall just as they entered the factory yard.

When Indigo arrived a minute later, he found the two tourists happily taking photographs of the geese. They could not understand why this small, thin, grey-haired boy came running in among them, crying out and flapping his arms wildly. They were even more surprised when the geese lifted like a great cloud into the air to reveal a spiky-haired girl lying rigid on the ground beneath them, her face frozen, her eyes wide in terror.

'Lucy!' Indigo threw himself down beside her. 'Are you OK?'

She began to shake violently. 'Beaks!' she cried, her eyes unfocused. 'Beaks!'

'It's OK, Lucy. It's over; they're gone.'

'Beaks!' she cried again. 'Beaks!'

'Call an ambulance, Polly,' said Indigo. 'Send it to the breadcrumb factory. I'm too late. She's in some kind of shock.'

The two Chinese tourists had wandered off at this point, and now a uniformed policeman appeared in the gateway, picked his way over the broken gates and paused in the yard, panting and out of breath. It had become quite dark and the policeman had to squint to see the figure crouched over the girl lying on the ground.

'You there,' he called breathlessly, 'what's going on?'

Chief Inspector Linus Milkweed of Blunt police had been in nearby Gob Street on police business when he heard the commotion and looked up to see the large yellow digger tearing up the busy street.

'Something's afoot!' he had cried and jogged off after it. Now, as the policeman regained his breath and came striding towards Indigo and Lucy, Indigo heard Polly's voice in his earpiece.

'The ambulance is on its way, Indigo. By remaining on the scene, you are significantly increasing your chances of taking the blame for what's happened.'

With that, Indigo got to his feet and turned towards the digger.

The policeman seemed to sense what was about to happen. 'You there! I command you to halt!'

'Beaks!' cried Lucy.

Indigo leaped from the front wheel of the digger to the bonnet to the roof to the wall. The policeman could only look on helplessly as he ran along the top of the wall like a cat.

Indigo sped up as he reached the end, leaped forward and, bringing his knees up to his chest, spun in mid-air – a manoeuvre which gave him enough momentum to get to the roof of the mitten factory across the road. He landed, rolled and rose to his feet in one fluid move, then jogged off across the roof. Behind him, the calls of the angry policeman grew more faint as Indigo reached the edge of the building, slid halfway down the drainpipe to the second-storey balcony, then threw himself across the street to the parapet of the opposite building. He skipped off across the roof.

So it was that Indigo McCloud left the forces of the law far behind him and, travelling across the roofs of Blunt, he came once more to the street on which he lived. He padded lightly across the top of the roof, and at Number 21 he slid carefully down the slates, grabbed the gutter and flipped neatly onto his window sill. He eased up the sash window noiselessly and slipped into his bedroom.

2

The Teatime Gathering
of the McCloud Family

Indigo McCloud's room was small and sparsely furnished. There was a narrow bed with a milk-crate nightstand. A card table – where he did his homework – stood by the opposite wall. A bookshelf alongside was home to a collection of tatty paperbacks, most with faded or broken spines. Indigo McCloud liked to reread his favourite books more than he liked to discover new ones.

There was other evidence in his room of his fondness for old things. His books shared the shelf with his oldest toy – a little red racing car, the wheels of which were slightly buckled. The lamp on his nightstand was made from a bottle that someone had covered in seashells. Indigo had found it in an abandoned yard and brought it home for Polly to fix. The radio had come from a skip. Polly had brought it back to life too.

The carpet had once been multi-coloured; thin lines of orange, red, green and blue had run from door to window, but years of traffic up and down the room had exposed the grey thread underneath. Now you could only see colour where the carpet disappeared under the bed.

There was a clatter of pans on the stove in the kitchen downstairs. Indigo sniffed the air and smelled the familiar smell of his father's cooking, a mixture of garlic and burning grass. He lingered a moment longer, listening, but the only sounds were cooking sounds. He and his father were alone in the house.

Indigo pulled off his black aviator jacket and was about to hang it on the nail on the back of his door when he saw that he had somehow managed to damage it. Frayed threads hung from a tear at the shoulder. Indigo frowned at the rip, trying to think how it had happened. In his head, he reran his pursuit of Lucy and the subsequent flight from the policeman. Did he snag his shoulder on something sharp? Some metal edge as he leaped from the yellow digger to the wall? Must have.

'Nuts,' said Indigo. He liked that jacket.

He now took a deep breath and prepared to go downstairs. His shoulders dropped. The cat-like poise with which he had scampered over the roofs of Blunt disappeared and was replaced by a graceless unease. Indigo glanced at the mirror on his bedroom door. A grey-haired boy stared back at him, wearing an expression that seemed to anticipate terrible things.

He opened the door of his bedroom and made his way down the rickety stairs to the kitchen, which was enveloped in clouds of steam. Tim McCloud, Indigo's father, was just about visible at the stove. He wore a voluminous multi-coloured jumper and his long legs terminated in a pair of bright yellow flip-flops. He liked to wear rubber gloves when he cooked. He disliked tying up his long grey hair, so when he worked at the stove, he often gave the appearance of an unkempt wizard struggling with a particularly difficult spell.

'Hiho, Indy!' Tim beamed at his son. 'Wait till you taste this!' He drew the large soup ladle from the steaming pot and slurped noisily at the gloopy green substance inside. 'Mmmm!' he said approvingly. 'Not bad, if I say so myself!'

Indigo took his place at the rough wooden table.

'Don't know where those girls are,' said Tim. 'Shouldn't be long, though! You know, Indy, I was thinking.' Tim came and stood behind his son's chair. 'Why don't you come along to my yoghurt-tasting class on Tuesday evening? I mean, you can't sit up there in that room all your life. You need to get out – you need to live a little! Some of these yoghurts are really quite something. Why, only the other night we tasted this cheeky little strawberry –'

Before he could continue, Indigo and his father were interrupted by the sound of bickering just outside the front door. A key turned in the lock and Indigo's ten-year-old twin sisters came into the kitchen.

'Chicken!' Root snarled at Berry.

'Egg!' Berry snarled back.

'CHICKEN!' Root elbowed her sister in the ribs.

'EGG!' Berry kicked Root in the shin.

The girls did not look anything alike. Root was small for her age and wore heavy wire braces over teeth that were quite badly misshapen. Her untidy hair refused to be tamed but stuck out at angles. Berry, significantly taller than her sister, kept her hair short and always wore grease-stained blue overalls. She wore a thin woollen glove on her left hand. The little finger of this glove was tied in a neat knot. The finger itself had been lost when one of Berry's engineering experiments – involving a bag of walnuts and a snapping turtle – had gone badly wrong.

Root and Berry were rarely seen apart and bickered constantly.

'Come on, girls, give it a rest!'

Tim turned from the stove but then started backwards in fright. 'Su! How many times have I told you not to sneak up on me like that!'

Su McCloud could move with the stealth of a cat and had succeeded in opening the front door and taking her place at the table without anyone noticing. She was rarely seen out of her school uniform and was the smallest of the McCloud siblings. Su had jet-black hair cut into a severe bob that framed a face notable for its one green and one blue eye. She was a black belt in karate and had won so many competitions that there were few flat surfaces in either the kitchen or the living room on which at least one of her trophies did not sit. A mismatched line of them was ranged along the top of the cooker.

All families have secrets, and the McClouds were no different. Few people knew, for example, that Su's full name was Tsunami, a name her parents had chosen because they mistakenly believed that it was Japanese for 'ocean wave'. In reality, of course, the name has come to mean 'tidal wave'.

A loud hiss made the children look up.

'Oh, bother!' said their father.

The large pot that had been bubbling on the stove had boiled over, covering the hob with frothy green bubbles. Now another key turned in the lock and the door opened again. Out on the street, a high sing-song voice was heard.

'Good evening, Mrs Oskins! What a beautiful evening, don't you think? Tell Dilly I said hello, won't you? Can't wait to see her at school tomorrow! Bye! Have a super-lovely evening!'

At the sound of this voice, something peculiar happened to Indigo McCloud. Unnoticed by either his sisters or his father, he seemed to shrink slightly. He seemed somehow to blend into his dingy surroundings. He was suddenly less *there* than he had been moments before.

The owner of the voice was Indigo's eldest sister, Peaches. As soon as she bid goodbye to Mrs Oskins, she entered the house, closed the door and came skipping into the kitchen.

'Hello, everyone! Sorry I'm late! But guess what? I sold two more calendars today – isn't that super? I think if I work really hard and really apply myself, I have a great chance of selling the most and winning that bike. Gosh! I'm not being arrogant, am I, Dad?' Peaches McCloud danced over to her father and gave him a hug.

'You? Arrogant?' He beamed at the others. 'I think we can safely say that our Peaches doesn't have an arrogant bone in her body. Now sit down, darling, dinner's ready.'

Peaches McCloud was by any standards a very pretty girl. Her features included a small nose which was ever-so-slightly upturned and which turned up a little more when she smiled. Her hair was arranged in waves of neat blond curls that fell gently on her shoulders. Her eyes were clear and blue and conveyed nothing but happiness and innocence. Peaches liked pretty things: kittens, ribbons, frills, cushions, sugar plums and so on. She dressed with exceptional style and carried herself with supreme confidence. The red velvet dress which she wore as she skipped gracefully about could hardly have been more at odds with the McClouds' grotty little kitchen, but Peaches seemed completely unaware of this.

'Oh, guess what, everybody!' She grinned excitedly at her siblings. 'There's a new family in Number 43! They're called the Tripes, and they have two children. Oswald is your age, Indy, and Mandy is the exact same age as me! Isn't that just super-great? I think I'll pop round to say hello after tea and give them a real Peaches McCloud welcome!'

As Peaches took her seat at the table, Tim lifted the huge pot from the stove and flip-flopped through the steam.

'Now, kids!' he said. 'I've got a special treat this evening! I've taken the nettle goulash that you all love and given it a new twist. This is nettle goulash with dandelion and garlic relish!'

He began ladling the thick, strong-smelling substance into all of the bowls on the table.

'Oh, Su,' said Tim, 'I nearly forgot.'

He replaced the large pot on the stove, fetched a plate from the oven and placed it before Su. It contained plain rice mixed with fish heads, which was the only thing that Su ever ate.

As she picked up her chopsticks and the others picked up their spoons and began to eat, Indigo watched them carefully through the steam. He could detect nothing out of the ordinary, nothing to suggest that any one of them had recently been involved in a high-speed race through the streets of Blunt. He watched Berry's gloved hand raise the spoon to her lips. Were those beads of sweat at her hairline?

'TRUCK!' Tim McCloud, who had been about to sit down, jumped up suddenly.

The entire family sprang into action around him. The twins leaped from the table and ran to the wall cupboard where the plates and cups were stored. As a hollow rumbling sound began to build outside, they placed themselves at either end of the cupboard and, holding the doors closed, hugged it tight. The hollow rumble stopped being a mere sound at this point and became a vibration that Indigo could feel rising up from the stone floor beneath him. Su snatched up the cut-glass trophy she had received the year before in the Under-11 regional mixed martial arts championship. Peaches reached for the mirror on the wall; Indigo ran for a framed picture of his mother which hung alongside it. As the vibrations became more intense and the windows began to rattle, Tim half-ran, half-stumbled for the fireplace and gathered up the small brown jar from the mantel. It was an urn with a small gold-coloured plastic nameplate on which the word 'Mary' had been written in swirly black letters.

Now the vibrations reached their highest point and the kitchen darkened as a huge articulated lorry, decorated with pictures of plastic Christmas trees, thundered along the cobbles outside. The cutlery in the drawer rattled, the glasses in the cupboard book-ended by the twins clinked, the staircase creaked and groaned and Indigo felt his bones tremble. The ground beneath him seemed to shift and the thin crack which ran up the kitchen wall snaked a little higher. The McClouds froze at their stations, clinging to their breakables as the truck moved on and the vibrations subsided. Once the danger had passed, Indigo carefully replaced the framed picture of his mother on the wall. It showed a pretty young woman laughing, her dark hair untidily tied up, her blue eyes shining brightly.

Tim McCloud did not return the urn to its place straight away, but cradled it, rubbing a thumb across the nameplate, before settling it reverentially on the mantel.

'Oh, Daddy!' Peaches turned, ran over and threw her arms around him. 'We all miss Mum so much!'

The children's mother had been taken from the McClouds some years earlier in an unfortunate accident which the family rarely talked about. When they did, they referred to it as 'The Incident'.

Indigo, now back at the table, looked over at his eldest sister. She was looking up at her father lovingly, her blond hair framing a face that was the picture of compassion and sweetness.

This, in fact, was exactly the pose she had struck for the official portrait that had been commissioned when she was given the 'Blunt Young Person of the Year' award a few weeks earlier.

The selection committee had sent a camera crew around to Adenoid Terrace ahead of the ceremony in order to make a commemorative video. They'd interviewed many of Peaches's neighbours in order to find out how everyone felt about her.

Mrs Coote lived at Number 61. Her eyes lit up at the mention of Peaches's name. 'Such a delightful girl!' she said.

Mr Kowalski from Number 40 agreed. 'Peaches is just the most thoughtful child,' he said, 'and such a wonderful influence on our Lulu.'

In fact, all of the parents interviewed had similar things to say about Peaches McCloud.

And when the camera crew spoke to the children of Adenoid Terrace about Peaches, they too were fulsome in their praise.

'Oh, yeah, Peaches is the best. She'd do anything for you.'

'Peaches is brilliant fun, and so nice!'

'We love Peaches – she's terrific.'

When the tapes of these interviews were played back at city hall, no-one among the selection committee noticed that the children's eyes did not light up when they talked about Peaches. Nobody noticed their clenched fists and twitching eyebrows. Nobody noticed that the children stumbled over their answers or that they looked around nervously when they spoke.

Nobody realised that they were all lying.

3

The Unfortunate Incident
with the Porridge

As soon as dinner was over and the dinner things were washed, dried and put away, Peaches made good her intention and left Number 21 to walk the short distance to Number 43 to pay a visit to the Tripes, who had just moved to Blunt. She was accompanied by all three of her sisters.

'Hello, Mandy!' said Peaches cheerily as Mandy Tripe opened the door. 'The girls and I just popped round to say hello and welcome you to Adenoid Terrace. Can we come in? Just for a teensy-weensy minute?'

Mandy was a tall, serious girl. Like her parents and her little brother Oswald, she had a dome of thick chestnut-coloured curls. She regarded Peaches and her sisters uncertainly. 'There's no-one here but me,' she said.

'Super!' said Peaches, stepping into the hallway.

Mandy stood aside as all four McCloud girls trooped past her into the living room. This room was similar in many ways to the McClouds' living room, except that where one was cluttered with the many sporting trophies that Su had won, the other was crammed with all sorts of bric-à-brac, including fake plants, matching place mats, clockwork mice, funny hats, figurines, coloured bottles, ceramic cats and novelty keyrings. No fewer than eight ornamental snow globes sat side by side on the mantelpiece.

The Tripe parents, Leonora and Bill, were reckless spendthrifts with a particular fondness for tacky souvenirs. They had moved to Adenoid Terrace following a failed business venture, the latest in a long line of failed business ventures.

Root, Berry and Tsunami arranged themselves behind Peaches as she drew to a halt on the carpet. Mandy followed them all into her living room and, as she did so, she felt the temperature drop suddenly. The smile which Peaches had worn at the door faded away. The eyes that had sparkled, that moments before had communicated nothing but warmth and welcome, slowly went dull. Peaches now looked about the room with the dead-eyed stare of a large predatory animal.

Mandy saw the look, and those of smirking menace on the faces of the other three girls. This confused her.

'Can I help you with something?' she asked.

At the sound of Mandy's voice, Peaches fixed her eyes upon her.

'SugarCool,' she said slowly. Turning, she swept her hand across the cushion of the most comfortable armchair in the living room and carefully sat down.

'Sorry?' said Mandy.

'Do you have any cans of SugarCool?' said Peaches, smoothing out her dress.

'Ah ... no,' said Mandy.

'Bobbity Bars?' Peaches rubbed the arm of the chair, then inspected her fingertips for dust.

'No,' said Mandy.

'You will need to get some in. You will need ... Root?'

The short, messy-haired Root produced a clipboard from under her arm and glanced down at it. 'Four Bobbity Bars and six cans of SugarCool per week,' she said.

'Four Bobbity Bars and six cans of SugarCool per week,' Peaches repeated. 'Someone will call for them every Monday morning. In addition, I will need a tray of ... Berry?'

'Cake pops,' said Berry.

Her twin sister elbowed her in the ribs. 'Caramel squares!'

'Cake pops!'

'Caramel squares!'

'I will need a tray of caramel squares the first Friday of each month,' said Peaches. 'Home-baked. Do not try to pass off some shop-bought junk as your own, or I shall find out. Do you understand?'

Mandy did not understand. 'I don't understand,' she said.

'The girls on this street like to give me things.' Peaches spoke as if each word was carefully polished before being allowed out; the corners of the consonants glittering coldly, like gemstones. 'They like to do this because when they don't, they find that bad things happen to them. You go to Cringegrot, do you not?'

Cringegrot was the name of Blunt's largest secondary school.

Mandy nodded.

'You will have seen Kirsty Rouse. You may not know her name but you will recognise her as the bald girl.'

Mandy nodded. She had seen the tall bald girl in school and had wondered about her.

There was a sudden burst of high-pitched laughter from Tsunami.

'Such a terrible accident,' said Peaches, though Mandy could not actually hear any concern for Kirsty in her voice. 'She didn't want to give me presents and then that happened to her. So unfortunate.'

'If I don't get you sweets …' said Mandy slowly, 'you'll shave my head?'

'Then there's Penny Milton,' said Peaches. 'She too decided that she didn't want to give me presents.'

'Penny Milton?' said Mandy. 'She's the one everyone says has a really hairy back.'

'Yes,' said Peaches slowly. 'Someone hacked into the hospital computer, raided her medical records and then published them online.'

'Heh heh heh heh heh.' This time, the laugh, which sounded like a machine gun being shot into a bag of cushions, came from Root. She grinned an unpleasant, crooked-toothed grin.

Mandy was horrified. 'You mean –' she began.

'Do you have any nasty little secrets, Mandy?' said Peaches, raising one delicate eyebrow.

'No. I mean, I –'

'Monday morning,' Peaches said, interrupting her. 'No later. Now. Souvenir calendars. You are a girl scout, are you not?'

'Yes.'

'From now on, you will need to sell fourteen per week. Root, give Mandy her map.'

Root unclipped a laminated page from her clipboard and handed it to Mandy. 'Her area is Cracker Street to the canal,' said Root.

'Your area is from Cracker Street to the canal,' said Peaches. 'Do not let me hear of you attempting to sell anywhere else.'

'What?' said Mandy, who was beginning to wonder if this was some kind of joke.

'All calendars are to be sold on the account of Peaches McCloud,' Peaches went on. 'If anyone asks, you are to say that I am a dear friend who has fallen ill and who you are helping meet her commitments. Do you understand?'

Mandy Tripe did not understand. 'I don't understand,' she said.

Peaches stood up. 'Fourteen per week until the bike is awarded. Cracker Street to the canal. It is very simple. You will do as I ask.'

'I can't sell calendars for you. I need to sell them for myself.'

Peaches said nothing for a moment. She continued to stare at Mandy with the same dead-eyed glare.

'Is there something you fear particularly, Mandy?' she asked quietly.

'Wh-what?'

'Snakes, perhaps? Rats? Spiders? Everyone fears something.' Now Peaches spoke very slowly, with long gaps between each word. 'Terrible things happen to girls who do not do as they are told. They step into the street at the wrong moment.' Peaches's eyes suddenly widened. 'And … dreadful things happen.'

Lesser girls would probably have crumbled at this point, but Mandy Tripe had spent most of her life trying to keep her parents from plunging the family into financial disaster. Over the years, her mother and father had run a chicken farm and two guesthouses into the ground. Their kettle-descaling service, soft-cheese delivery business, hamster beauty parlour and ukulele rental shop had all failed, one after the other. They had a dream that some day they would be highly successful business people, that they would drive expensive cars and wear expensive clothes. At night, after the children had gone to bed, Leonora and Bill would pretend that they were being interviewed on TV about their success; each parent would take it in turn to be the interviewer.

It was a difficult life for Mandy and her brother, Oswald, who would lie awake at night, listening to their parents downstairs, and wonder whether there would be enough to eat the next day.

That is why they took matters into their own hands. Their parents' latest venture was a flavoured-porridge shop, which they called Porridge Plus! Oswald worked there after school, where he did his best to stop his mother and father from ordering too much of the wrong kind of porridge or from taking money from the till to spend in the novelty egg-cup shop next door. Mandy, meanwhile, worked part time in the tweezers factory. She was also a girl scout, and for many months before she had come to Blunt, she too had been taking part in the competition to which Peaches had referred earlier. The girl scout who sold the most souvenir calendars would be awarded a brand-new bicycle. These calendars featured a range of local landmarks, including Cragmire's cow museum and, in Blunt, the Crappy Tower Interpretive Centre and floating sewage works. Mandy was determined to win the bike because she wished to supplement the family income with an early-morning paper round.

'I need that b-bike,' she blurted out, cracking her knuckles anxiously. 'I need it.'

There was a moment's silence, in which all four McCloud girls stared unblinking at Mandy.

'Su,' said Peaches, 'show Mandy what happens to girls who do not do as they are told.'

Su reached out and picked up the nearest thing to her, which happened to be a lime-green dining-room chair decorated with pink ribbons. She tossed this effortlessly into the air before her and, as it fell, she executed a series of karate moves with such speed that Mandy could not actually follow her hands. There was a smell of sawdust and a pile of lime-green sticks fell neatly onto the floor. Two pink ribbons floated down and landed gently on top of them.

Mandy did not know any kung fu, had never boxed or taken self-defence classes. If Su were to pick her up by the ankles and bang her head repeatedly on the floor, there would be nothing she could do about it. But Mandy Tripe had a secret weapon.

Her scream.

She could scream longer and louder than almost anyone else, and the pitch of that scream was such that her parents had expressly forbidden her to scream anywhere near the house. This was because whenever she did, glass would break.

But now, without further ado, Mandy Tripe opened her mouth and began to scream.

It was a truly terrible sound. High and whiny and so incredibly loud that scientists at the earthquake monitoring station in the nearby town of Bulstrode registered it on their equipment. One by one, the eight ornamental snow globes on the mantelpiece exploded, sending little showers of water and confetti into the air. Every dog within a three-mile radius stood up and began barking.

The McCloud girls could do nothing but run from the living room with their hands clamped about their ears.

Mandy's scream coincided with her brother Oswald's return from the porridge shop with a large pot of mackerel-flavoured porridge, which his parents had made up but had been unable to sell. Oswald planned to heat it up for the family's supper. He was standing outside the door, fumbling for his key, when Peaches came rushing out of the house and collided with him. The pot flew upwards, turned over and emptied itself all over Peaches's blond ringlets and beautiful red velvet dress. To complete her indignity, the pot then landed, with a quiet squelch, on her head.

At this point, several adults emerged from their houses, all drawn by Mandy's scream. They arrived just in time to see Peaches, full to the brim with murderous rage, pulling the pot from her head. But when she looked up to see half a dozen pairs of eyes staring at her with a mixture of confusion and concern, her demeanour changed instantly.

'Oh, dear!' she said brightly, as globules of fish-scented porridge slid from her head to her shoulders. 'What a silly accident! But don't worry about me, Oswald. Mandy seems a little distressed; you'd better go and look after your sister.'

The adults rushed over to help Peaches.

'Are you OK, dear?'

'Would you like a towel?'

'What a curious smell!'

Flanked by her sisters, still dripping great grey globs of porridge, Peaches was helped back to her house by a small gaggle of concerned adults.

4

The Lonely Rebellion
of Lucy Jones

While the McCloud girls were calling on Mandy Tripe that evening, Indigo made his way across the roofs to the hospital on Pox Street with the intention of checking in on Lucy, but a nurse told him that she remained paralysed by shock and could not have visitors. As he turned to go, he heard a cry from the ward behind him.

'The beaks! THE BEAKS!'

As he walked slowly back to Adenoid Terrace, his mind returned, as it had so often in the past week, to something that had happened in school earlier that month.

He had been making his way along the corridor between classes when Lucy stepped out of a doorway and blocked his path.

'Hello, Indigo,' she said.

'Hi,' said Indigo, and moved to go around her. Lucy stepped sideways to block him.

'I'd like to talk to you.'

As well as short spiky hair, Lucy had eyes of a very deep, penetrating blue. The knot of her school tie hung loose below her collar. Her jumper was several sizes too big and she wore it with the sleeves rolled up, giving the impression that if a fight were to break out she would be ready. She looked at Indigo now with a slight smile on her face. Indigo was used to smiles like this, smiles that were faintly mocking. He waited for her eyes to flick upwards to his grey hair, for her to make some comment about it.

'I need your help.'

'What?'

'Your help. I need it.'

The idea of Lucy asking for his help was so far from what he'd expected from her that he could only repeat himself. 'What?'

'It's Peaches.'

Indigo felt himself colouring. He gritted his teeth to try and make it stop but knew there was no point. He cleared his throat. 'I'm sure Peaches would be only too happy to help you.'

'No, no, no.' Lucy stepped closer and her voice dropped. 'It's about Peaches. I need to talk to you *about* Peaches.'

'Lucy, I –'

She cut across him. 'You know how many of the kids in my class are selling calendars for her? Do you? I'll tell you. All of them. That's how many. Even the boys. And if you don't meet your quota?' She drew a finger across her throat. 'You saw what she did to Kirsty Rouse and Penny Milton. That's just the beginning. I know it is. There's worse coming, Indigo, and you know it. I know you do. You've got to help, Indigo, you've just –'

Indigo pulled his arm away. 'Look,' he began, but before he could say more, Lucy whispered fiercely: 'There!' She gripped his wrist again, her gaze on something behind him. 'There she is.'

Indigo didn't turn around. 'Peaches?'

'Just coming out of class. That smile!' Lucy spat, still staring over his shoulder. 'So pure! So innocent! You'd think she wouldn't hurt a fly!'

'I gotta go.' Indigo wrenched away and strode past Lucy.

'Indigo, please! We've got to strike back! We've got to do something! Come on.' She ran after him. 'Look, you don't have to do anything yourself, but give me something, anything ... Information! If I had information about her, something I could use.'

'I can't help you, Lucy.' He kept walking.

'I'm ... I'm on my own, Indigo.' Her voice had cracked. 'I'm the only one holding out. I won't sell for her – I won't do it.'

Indigo kept walking. He did not turn back.

In the days that followed, he had tried to convince himself that Peaches would not harm Lucy. He even began tailing his sisters when they left the house, following them from the roofs as they made their way through the streets of Blunt, but they never did anything to suggest they were planning a nasty surprise for anyone. He listened outside their bedroom door for hours and didn't hear so much as a whisper.

And yet he had known that evening that something bad was going to happen. He could taste it in the smoky air.

It was as if the accordions in the factory were playing a lament for Lucy and the donkeys in the sanctuary were singing along in time. But what had Indigo done? Nothing. He had dithered at Polly's window and done nothing – until it was too late.

A wave of guilt washed over him.

He decided against returning to his own house and went instead across the street to Polly's. There, he sat on her brown bedspread, surrounded by her brown walls, with his head in his hands.

'It's all my fault,' he said.

Polly regarded him expressionlessly. 'It was Peaches,' she said. 'Peaches, Su, Root and Berry. The geese fly over at the same time every year. Peaches timed the attack with the digger so that Lucy would be covered in breadcrumbs at exactly the right time.'

Indigo did not reply.

'Perhaps we should go to the police, Indigo,' said Polly.

'And tell them what? That a girl everyone thinks is an angel terrorised Lucy with geese?'

'So, what should we do?'

'If I had helped her,' he said quietly, 'none of this might have happened.'

Polly, her hands flat on her lap, stared at her friend as if he were a puzzle that she was on the point of solving.

'That may be true,' she said eventually.

'Thanks, Polly,' said Indigo flatly, 'thanks.'

'Why are you thanking me? I have not given you anything.'

'It's sarcasm, Polly.'

'Sarcasm,' said Polly. 'Of course. I've read about that.' She blinked twice and stared at Indigo. 'I heard a joke today, Indigo. About an unhappy mole and a bar of lemon soap. Would you like to hear it?'

'No, Polly, I wouldn't.'

'This is because you feel guilty about your role in what happened to Lucy Jones.'

'Yes.'

'I've read about that too,' said Polly. 'A recent paper in the *Journal of Applied Psychology* found that feelings of guilt are frequently associated with –'

'Polly,' Indigo said, 'now would be a good time to talk about ducks.'

'Certainly, Indigo,' said Polly, and without hesitation she began: 'There are well over one hundred species of duck, all of which are omnivorous. In addition to eating fish and crustaceans, they will also forage for insects, seeds and fruit. The duck has been domesticated for more than two and a half thousand years.'

Polly loved ducks. She also loved talking about ducks. Most people found the subject boring, but Indigo did not. In fact, whenever Indigo was troubled or upset, he would ask Polly to talk about ducks. It was a ritual that originated in their very first meeting, many years earlier. For whatever reason, hearing his friend discuss her favourite subject gave Indigo a certain relief. And Polly, who had never lost her fascination with ducks, was always glad to oblige.

Now, as she went on and on about Muscovy ducks, Dendermonde ducks and German Pekin ducks, Indigo stood up and went to the window. Outside, the few streetlights that were still working glowed weakly in the darkness. A thin drizzle began to fall on Adenoid Terrace. With its broken cobbles, cracked windows and missing roof slates, it could hardly have looked any worse. But it was home. His home.

He looked over at Lucy's window and, as he did, another wave of guilt began to build and rush towards him. This had happened time and again over the past few hours, and each time these waves of guilt washed over him, they had uncovered a heart strewn with soft squidgy things. Things like sorrow, sadness and regret. This time, however, as Indigo stared out into his unlovely street, he found that the wave had uncovered a new, unfamiliar emotion. It was harder than the others, and darker, and had more edges. It took him a moment to identify it.

Anger.

That's what it was. Small and dark and hard and real. Anger.

He looked up. 'No more,' said Indigo quietly.

Polly stopped talking. 'Pardon?' she said.

'No more, Polly,' said Indigo. 'I'm not going to stand by while she terrorises anyone else. I'm going to stop her. I'm going to stop Peaches.'

5

The Secret World
of the McCloud Girls

The following morning, the McClouds' kitchen was as chaotic as usual. Su was eating her fish heads and rice at the table. Root had her laptop open. Her small dark eyes were fixed on the screen and her fingers were a blur on the keyboard.

Berry, her face stained with oil, was equally intent on the small electric motor at which she worked. Her small dark eyes – the only physical characteristic she shared with her twin – narrowed as she wrestled with the motor, trying to remove one of the two half-rusted bolts that held the rotor in position. As Indigo passed silently behind them and took his place at the breakfast table, she pulled too hard – the nut came flying off and zipped through the air. Without looking up from her meal, Su caught it in her chopsticks and lowered it onto the table.

Berry, now intent on the second bolt, did not notice. Once again, however, she pulled too hard with her gloved hand and a second nut came flying off. This one struck her twin on the forehead.

'Watch what you're doing, you idiot!' Root barked and, grabbing her sister's nose, she gave it a vicious tug.

Berry yelped and seized Root's nose in her knuckles and jerked it forward. Root squealed. Both now stood at the table, holding each other's noses.

'Let go!' said Root in a nasal whine.

'You first!' Berry whined back.

As the twins squabbled on, Peaches emerged from the bathroom in a Dalmatian-patterned bathrobe with her hair wrapped up in a matching towel.

'Hiho, darling,' said Tim, turning from the stove with a large pot of porridge. 'Have you got rid of the smell?'

'I think so, Daddy,' said Peaches, as she pulled out a chair and sat down. 'What a silly accident. I'm only glad that no-one else got hurt.'

Tim frowned and shook his head. 'I don't know, Peaches,' he said. 'I mean, you and the girls were so kind-hearted to go over there to welcome those children, and what do you get in return? A pot of porridge over the head. I'm not so sure I should be quite so forgiving in your shoes. What if it had been hot porridge? Have you thought of that? That boy needs to be more careful.' He gestured with the ladle, and a thick gloop of porridge flew from its end. Tim's glasses were still steamed up from the stove and he did not see it, but the children watched the tennis-ball-sized globule arc through the air and land with a heavy, wet sound on the wall, where it stuck hard. 'That must be the sixth time you've had to wash your hair and all because of a boy who doesn't know how to handle porridge,' he said.

'Oh, not to worry, Daddy!' said Peaches. 'It was just a silly accident. Nothing to get upset about.'

Indigo slipped unnoticed out of the house before everyone else, but he did not go to school. Halfway there, he stopped, took to the roofs and quickly returned to Adenoid Terrace. He flipped soundlessly back into his bedroom and hovered there, listening to the sounds of his sisters leaving the house, one after the other. Su had already left – he had seen her on the road. Now, through the open window, he heard Root and Berry emerge onto the pavement below.

'Let go!'

'You let go!'

Peaches now exited her room and skipped down the stairs. As he listened, he looked down at his palms, which glistened with sweat. His insides felt as though they had been hollowed out.

Downstairs, he heard Peaches sing out a happy 'Goodbye' to their father.

'Just a tick, Peaches,' his father called back. 'I'll walk a bit of the way with you – I need to go to the market.'

Moments later, they both left. The front door slammed shut. Indigo listened until the sound of his father's feet slapping the footpath faded away, leaving the house in complete silence. Then he stood up, silently opened his bedroom door and stepped out into the hall.

He stared at his sisters' door, then took a deep breath and placed his hand on the doorknob, feeling the terrible uncertainty of a bomb-disposal expert who can't remember if he should cut the blue or the red wire.

He turned the handle.

The room was small and cluttered and was mostly taken up with two sets of bunk beds, which were crammed against the walls and separated only by a shabby pink dressing table, whose top was covered with an assortment of things, including hair accessories, little jars and bottles, postcards and a large hardback book entitled *All New Kittens in Ribbons – So Cute You'll Just Die!* The floor was strewn with bits of metal, wires, screws, pulleys and ropes – the leftovers from whatever Berry had been making – while the shelves were crowded with Su's trophies and rosettes, as well as photographs of the girls involved in their various hobbies.

Taking great care to remember the placement of everything he moved, Indigo slowly began searching the room. He was not sure exactly what it was he was looking for, but he knew he would recognise it when he saw it.

He found Root's laptop and turned it on, then spent twenty fruitless minutes trying to access the files on the machine.

The drawers of the dressing table revealed nothing of interest.

Indigo got down on all fours and began groping under the bed, but all he found were empty SugarCool cans and Bobbity Bar wrappers. In fact, the area under the beds was full of rubbish. Only one small section, right at the end of Root's bed, was clear.

He bent down and inspected this area again, but could see nothing of note. It was only when he reached under the bed that his hand came on something fixed to the base, which felt, for all the world, like a handle. Closing his fingers about it, he pulled. It came back fluidly and quietly and, as it did, a very odd thing happened.

The pink dressing table slid forward and to the side, revealing a small circular opening in the floor, with steps that led downwards. Indigo allowed himself only a moment to stare, then took another deep breath, carefully stepped around the dressing table and began descending what turned out to be a narrow spiral staircase. It wound down for about two and a half storeys before terminating in a large open space.

Indigo McCloud stood at the bottom of the stairs and looked around. 'Wow!' he whispered.

The room was bright, white and spotlessly clean. It made him think of a laboratory. It was also large and must, he thought, extend beyond their house and continue under Number 23 next door.

'That's why I heard nothing when I listened at the door,' he said quietly to himself. 'They were all down here.'

There was a whiteboard at one end, which ran the length of the wall. At one side of this board, someone had drawn what appeared to be a map of Blunt, with arrows marking many of the streets.

Along another wall there was a workbench fronted by an array of small drawers. Each one was carefully labelled: *size 4 screws*, *13a fuses*, *lug wrenches*, *sprockets*, *electronic components* and so on. A curious-looking mechanical contraption sat alone on the workbench. Indigo hovered over it, trying to figure out what it was for without actually touching it. A small silver ball was lodged at the head of a little chute, at the end of which a lever operated a hammer on a tiny spring, which was poised above a series of cogwheels. It appeared to Indigo as if Berry's strange machine – it had to be Berry's – was some kind of insanely complicated mousetrap.

He left it and moved silently about the room, past filing cabinets, a bank of humming computers and a large vending machine, which was stocked entirely with Bobbity Bars and cans of SugarCool.

Two large squashy sofas stood in one corner, facing a huge pink and white easy chair.

As Indigo surveyed the room, something caught his eye, something over by the whiteboard. Something orange. He moved swiftly towards it and plucked it from the board. It was a small piece of paper with writing on it: a list, written on – he sniffed – peach-scented notepaper, decorated with teddy bears clutching love hearts.

When Indigo got to school later that morning, he found it impossible to concentrate. His mind kept returning to the slip of paper he had seen pinned to the whiteboard. There were three names on it. The first was Lucy Jones. This had been crossed out in heavy black marker. The second two names on Peaches McCloud's peach-scented hit list had not been crossed out. They were Mandy and Oswald Tripe.

6

The Sudden Descent
of the Traffic Cone

'OK, Polly,' said Indigo, 'what have you got?'

They were back in Polly's brown bedroom. She hit a button on the computer and the scrolling lines of type on the screen were immediately replaced with a photograph of Mandy Tripe, who stared nervously out from under her dome of chestnut curls.

'Mandy Jessica Tripe,' said Polly, 'is 1.524 metres tall. She is a member of Blunt Majorettes and hates the smell of tinned pineapple. Her shoe size is four and a half, though she takes a size five in runners. When nervous, she has a habit of cracking her knuckles. She doesn't own any yellow socks or red T-shirts and is terrified of spiders. Her cousin Larry has never been on a rollercoaster. She doesn't have any pets, but if she did, it would be either a cat called Binky or a stick insect called Sarge. She pronounces the word "cousin" like this: "cousint". Her mother thinks she's allergic to kangaroo droppings –'

'Polly –' said Indigo quietly.

Polly went on: 'But she isn't really. Her father's sister

Bertha once stole an organic chicken from Tesco and his other sister Shirley once burned her elbow –'

'Polly!' said Indigo.

Polly stopped abruptly and turned to look at him. 'Yes, Indigo?'

'Where did you get all that?'

Polly blinked twice and placed her hands flat on her lap. 'From a variety of sources. Do you wish me to list those sources?'

Indigo shook his head slowly. 'No. That's fine, thanks, Polly.'

'You're welcome.'

Indigo stood up. 'Now, Mandy was first on the list, so Peaches'll probably go for her first. Blunt Majorettes, you said?'

'Yes. Her uniform has one missing button on the left-hand side of her tunic. Rehearsals are on Tuesday afternoons at five thirteen at the sports complex on Eek Street.'

Indigo began pacing behind Polly's chair. 'Lucy,' he said slowly, 'was attacked doing something that Peaches would have known about in advance. It would have been easy to find out that she was learning the mandolin. Easy too to find out exactly what time her lesson was on. Peaches will know all about the majorettes; she'll know –' Indigo stopped. 'What date is today?'

'Twenty-fourth of April.'

'Hang on, it's just five days to Ingratitude Day.'

'That is correct,' said Polly.

'The majorettes will be marching. They always do. Polly, see if you can pull up the parade route.'

It took less than twenty seconds for Polly to find what he was looking for. Mandy's face disappeared from the screen, to be replaced by a colour-coded map of Blunt. Sections of it, indicating the path of the parade, were greyed out.

'That's it,' said Indigo quietly. 'That's what I saw in their bunker. It's going to happen on the twenty-ninth, during the Ingratitude Day parade.'

'What is going to happen?'

Indigo shook his head. 'Don't know. Something bad.'

* * *

Ingratitude Day is one of the biggest holidays in Blunt's calendar. It celebrates the famous incident, in 1163, when King Norman the Norman visited Blunt and was so pleased with the industry of its citizens that he presented the town with a boot made of solid gold. On his way home, however, he realised that no-one had said 'Thanks,' so he returned to Blunt with the intention of taking the golden boot back. The town, however, refused to give it back, and so the king laid siege. That year, there had been a record beetroot harvest and the storehouses were full. After three weeks of trying to starve the town, Norman grew bored and gave up. He left without his golden boot.

On Ingratitude Day, the town celebrates its bad manners by reversing all the usual niceties. On Ingratitude Day, one friend might greet another with a new hairdo by saying, 'I see you've persuaded a flea-infested badger to live on your head. I wonder how he puts up with the smell?'

In response, the other person might say, 'Why don't you shut your trap, you wrinkly old pus bucket.'

A variety of ingratitude-related events are held throughout the day. There's an Insult Tournament where prizes are awarded for the longest, most appropriate and most imaginative insults. The Most Irritating Toddler and Ugly Baby competitions are always hugely popular. At the accompanying home and garden exhibition, prizes are awarded for the Blandest Cake and Most Unappealing Bunch of Parsnips.

The centrepiece of the day's events is the parade, when bands, floats, local teams and so forth make their way through the streets, throwing clods of dirt at people and carrying beautifully decorated signs saying things like: 'I hope you have a miserable Ingratitude Day, you shower of whingeing snot-gobblers.' People line the parade route hissing and shouting things like, 'You're rubbish!' or 'Call that a float?' or 'Come back next year when you've learned to play!'

All in all, it helps the people of Blunt get a lot of negativity out of their systems and the following day everything goes back to normal, and people who had called each other diseased dogs' bottoms and pimply sludge faces the day before greet each other warmly as they go about their daily business.

In the days leading up to the parade, Indigo and Polly spent hours trying to work out what Peaches intended for Mandy Tripe without any real success. When Polly tried to hack into Peaches's underground computer network, she found it completely locked down and utterly impenetrable. This, they both knew, was all down to Root.

'What are we going to do?' Polly asked.

'I'll follow Mandy tomorrow from the roofs. We'll stay in touch over the headsets. We can't let the girls know I'm onto them.'

* * *

At a quarter past eleven, just fifteen minutes before the parade was due to begin, a slight grey-haired figure, dressed in black, arrived unseen onto the roofs above Derange Street. Indigo looked down on the floats, bands and marchers as they began to assemble on the cobbles. Since it was a holiday, the Christmas-tree factory was only on half-time and the air in Blunt was unusually smoke-free.

Blunt Majorettes marched in three columns towards the head of the parade, with Mandy Tripe leading the left-most column. Holding her head of chestnut curls high, she wore a fixed smile and twirled her baton with obvious expertise.

Indigo, meanwhile, padded along the roofs of the buildings overhead, his eyes fixed to the top of Mandy's head.

For ten minutes, nothing of note happened. The bands marched, the floats shuffled, Mandy twirled and everyone along the route waved flags depicting the town crest (which featured a golden boot and a beetroot) and howled their disapproval.

Towards the end of Skidball Street stood a building encased in scaffolding. There had recently been a sweet-shop there, but it had been closed down the previous year by health inspectors when it was found to be infested with hordes of tiny black spiders. The site was then bought by a local businessman, Harold Cribbins, who began renovations with the intention of opening another of the many Humpty Depots that dotted the town. These shops sold novelty egg-cups and nothing else. The Tripes' shop adjoined one such depot in another part of town.

As the parade approached the building site, Indigo thought he noticed movement on the scaffolding across the street. He squinted but didn't see it again. Then he noticed the traffic cones. A row of them stood on the first floor of the scaffolding.

'Polly,' he said, 'why would anyone put traffic cones in a place where there was no traffic?'

'I don't know, Indigo.' Polly's voice crackled over the headset.

Indigo stared harder and once again thought he noticed movement in the gloom behind the cones.

'I think this could be it,' he said quietly. 'I think there's someone there.'

Then it happened.

One of the traffic cones dropped suddenly and swiftly and landed with a soft, sucking noise on Mandy's head.

7

The Voyage of
the Sludge Barge

Mandy dropped her baton, and her hands went to the cone, trying to prise it off, but it was stuck fast. She could not see, of course, so she stumbled forward, groping the air and calling for help.

In the general chaos of Ingratitude Day, everyone who saw the incident thought it was part of the festivities and good-naturedly shouted abuse at Mandy.

Indigo watched as she blundered about the parade, but at this stage, the majorettes had left her behind and the Christmas-tree factory float was passing the building site. This float showed the same scene it showed every year, which was Santa Claus in the bath, having his back scrubbed and hair washed by a large squadron of elves.

Mandy bounced off the float and went stumbling back into the building site, where she walked straight into the service elevator, colliding with the control panel at the back. Indigo watched the door of the metal cage shut and the lift begin to rise slowly. By the time he made it across the roofs to the top of the structure, Mandy's lift had reached the third storey.

'Mandy!' Indigo called. 'Mandy!'

Though he could see her through the steel grid-work beneath him, there was no obvious way down to her.

The lift opened its doors onto a narrow corridor, hemmed in by rough steel gates. Mandy went stumbling from one side to the next, groping and trying without success to pull the traffic cone from her head. She had also begun to scream, but the muffling effects of the traffic cone meant that she could not be heard above the noise and bustle of the parade.

Then Indigo saw where she was headed. At the end of the corridor was the upper end of a long plastic chute, which the builders used to dispose of rubble and other waste materials. It ran the length of the three storeys to the ground.

If Mandy stumbled into it – and that now seemed unavoidable – she would surely fall to her death.

'Mandy!' Indigo called again. 'Mandy! You have to stop! Wait there! Wait!'

In her panic, and with the cone clamped so tightly about her head, Mandy could hear nothing. Indigo darted about the roof, frantically trying to see how he might get down to her, but the way was barred by a lattice-work of steel. He peered over the edge of the roof and saw that the disposal chute led directly to a large yellow skip. Brown tarpaulin was strapped tightly across its top.

'If she hits that …' Indigo began, then stopped and stood up, surveying the town beneath him.

The building site backed onto the Pyewkenocky Canal, and at this moment, the sludge barge was making its way slowly in Indigo's direction, bound for the sludge works in the town of Mullet, eight kilometres away. A large grey horse was being led slowly along the towpath that ran alongside the canal. It was tethered by a long rope to the sludge-laden barge.

Indigo stared and began to understand.

'Polly!' he shouted into his headset. 'Bring up a bigger map. I need to know what's at the Elbow.'

Indigo ran, flipped over the edge of the roof, then began to make his way rapidly down the building, moving as quickly as he could from one window ledge to the one beneath it.

* * *

The Pyewkenocky Canal was built in 1845 by the little-known engineer Lloyd Peersbynt Flount to connect the River Blunt with the town of Mullet, which had a thriving sludge industry. Flount had been very active in the greater Blunt area during the 1840s and was also responsible for several of its other engineering curiosities. There was the floating sewage works on the east side of the town, and also the collapsible bridge, built for swift disassembly if the town was attacked.

Whereas both of these had been constructed with all due care and attention, Lloyd had badly miscalculated the route of the canal, taking it in a north-easterly direction, whereas Mullet actually lay to the north-west. By the time he realised his mistake, a mile of the canal had already been constructed, and the only solution was to turn through ninety degrees and continue in the correct direction. As a result, the canal, unlike most canals, features a tight, right-angled bend just outside the town. This bend is known locally as the 'Elbow'.

Indigo was halfway down the building when Mandy hit the chute and toppled in. He followed the half-muffled sounds of her screams as she fell, hit the tarpaulin-covered skip and bounced cleanly off, as if it were a trampoline. She rose into the air again and arced out over the canal, and would have splashed right into it if the barge had not been coming through right at that moment. Mandy Tripe landed with a splat into the middle of a large mound of black sludge.

The shock of the fall, the bounce and the sludge silenced her momentarily, but as Indigo reached the ground, she began to scream with renewed intensity. The traffic cone may have reduced the volume of these wails, but it also managed to make them weird, high pitched and insect-like.

At the sound of the impact, and of Mandy's distorted screams, the horse took off.

'Whoa, girl!' her handler yelled, but it was no use. The horse galloped away, dragging the sludge-filled barge with Mandy Tripe on top.

The ruins of the old town walls ran along the edge of the canal. They were uneven, rising to a height of six or seven metres at some points and falling almost to ground level at others. As horse and majorette accelerated off along the canal, Indigo climbed rapidly onto the walls and sprinted after them.

'The Elbow is home to two businesses,' came Polly's voice over the headset. 'There is a pillow factory on one side and on the other is Auntie Maggie's Big Hairy Spider Emporium.'

'What?' said Indigo

'The Elbow is home to two –'

Indigo cut her off. 'Auntie Maggie's Big Hairy Spider Emporium?'

'Yes. It opened on Friday. It features some of the world's largest, hairiest spiders.'

'Wait a second,' said Indigo. 'Spiders … That was one of the things you found out, wasn't it? Mandy is terrified of spiders, right?'

'That is correct,' said Polly.

'So that's where they're headed,' Indigo panted.

He felt for that little nugget of anger that he had uncovered a couple of days earlier. 'Not today, Peaches,' he said quietly, 'not today.'

'Is Peaches there, Indigo?' Polly asked.

'No, Polly, forget it.'

The Elbow lay a little way out of town. A horse, no matter how strong, can only pull a barge laden with sludge and topped with a squealing majorette so fast. Indigo calculated, not unreasonably, that if he could maintain a good sprint along the top of the old town wall, he would be able to catch up to the barge before it reached the Elbow.

'"There are no cages or glass enclosures in Auntie Maggie's Big Hairy Spider Emporium."' Polly was clearly reading from something. '"It is an open-air habitat in which the world's largest arachnids enjoy fresh air and wide open spaces where they can spin webs, climb trees, bask in the sunshine and sink their fangs into their prey and gorge on their blood in a family-friendly atmosphere."'

Now the signs for Auntie Maggie's Big Hairy Spider Emporium came into view. Indigo could see a low building surrounded by trees and assorted vegetation, and bordered by a tall fence. The barge had begun to scrape against the wall of the canal as the horse fought to escape the terrible wailing, which, despite the length of time it had been going on, seemed to Indigo to be getting shriller all the time.

When the horse reached the Elbow and turned sharply, the barge was whipped sideways and went sliding across the water. Indigo leaped from the wall just as the traffic-cone-topped Mandy and a good proportion of the sludge was catapulted into the air. As she went flying towards the top of the fence, it looked as if Peaches and her sisters had triumphed once again. Mandy, the girl who had defied Peaches, who had refused to sell calendars on her behalf, would find out, just as Lucy had, exactly what happens when you displease Peaches McCloud. The unfortunate girl would shortly land head first into her worst nightmare.

But it was not to be.

Indigo met Mandy in mid-air, deflecting her instead into the soft reeds and sedge that grew by the water. She flopped down into the weeds, leaped instantly to her feet and, with a huge effort, managed finally to prise the traffic cone from her head. Panting and wide-eyed, she took in her surroundings. The canal, the weeds, the disappearing horse, the half-emptied barge and the tall fence near which she had landed.

'Where am I?' she gasped, but there was no-one there to answer.

In pushing Mandy to safety, Indigo had deflected himself over the top of the fence and into Auntie Maggie's Big Hairy Spider Emporium.

It was Ingratitude Day, so the emporium was closed for the morning while everyone went to see the parade. Indigo landed like a cat, rolled over and froze.

There, on a large rock in front of him, just centimetres from his face, stood the largest, hairiest spider that Indigo had ever seen. Each of its legs was as thick as his thumb. Its body was large, black, bristling and marked with dark green stripes. All of its eight glassy eyes regarded Indigo expressionlessly. One of its fangs twitched.

'Polly,' said Indigo quietly, 'I'm going to describe a spider to you. I want you to tell me if it is poisonous or not. OK?'

'OK, Indigo.'

Indigo quickly and carefully described the spider, which continued to stare blankly at him.

'That is a Harmless dancing spider,' said Polly.

'OK,' said Indigo, relaxing slightly. 'That's good. It's harmless.'

'No. It's called after Sir Arthur Harmless, who wrote about it in his travel book *Various Animals That Have Tried to Kill Me*. Its bite, while not usually fatal, is exceptionally painful.'

'I see,' said Indigo.

'It's important that you make no sudden moves,' said Polly. 'And most of all, if it starts dancing, you need to –'

It was at this point that Polly's voice died abruptly.

'What?' Indigo whispered. 'Polly? What is it?'

Raising his hand slowly, his eyes still on the spider, Indigo adjusted the headset and called again for his friend. No sound emerged from the earpiece.

Now the Harmless dancing spider began to dance – slowly at first, flexing its thick black legs first one way, then another. It grooved back and forth on its rock, dipping its fangs, twirling its legs and swaying its green-striped body as it moved.

'Polly?' Indigo whispered again, his eyes fixed on those of the great hairy spider as it sped up, kicking out its legs, raising its fangs in the air and executing a clever back-flip.

Polly did not reply. The headset had failed.

What she would have told Indigo, if communications had not broken down, was that Harmless dancing spiders hunt in packs, and that while one distracts the prey with its dancing display, others sneak around the back to attack. So it was that as Indigo watched the spider moonwalk across the top of its rock, no less than four other Harmless dancing spiders leaped from neighbouring rocks. One landed on Indigo's neck and another on his shoulder, while the last two pounced on his left leg. All four sank their fangs into him simultaneously.

Indigo cried out. Leaping and spinning about, he managed to dislodge them. They tumbled onto the sand and scuttled away. Indigo, frantically swiping at his body to remove any spiders that might still be clinging to him, made straight for the fence and scrambled up. Swinging his legs over the top, he landed in the weeds where Mandy Tripe had fallen some minutes earlier.

Mandy, relatively unscathed by her ordeal with the traffic cone and sludge, had, at this stage, made her way back to town. This meant that there was no-one there to see a slight boy with grey hair stumbling along the edge of the canal, holding his neck and grimacing in pain.

No-one saw him fall to the ground, where he remained, kneeling and gritting his teeth, until the agony became too much and he passed out.

8

The Unexpected Bravery of Polly Mole

The McClouds had not always lived on Adenoid Terrace. When Indigo was small, they lived with six other families on a farm in the Spink Valley, some eighty kilometres from the town of Blunt. This was before the terrible incident which was to deprive the McClouds of their mother. Back then, Tim and Mary McCloud believed that children should grow up in a place where you did not need money, where you could grow all your own food, make all your own clothes and live close to nature, among the trees, birds, flowers and so forth.

Unfortunately, the Spink Valley was a cold, inhospitable place, where the crows stole the cutlery, the goats ate the washing and the cows were vicious and gave little milk. A bitter wind would sweep down from the mountains, creating monstrous snowdrifts during the winter and great clouds of dust during the summer. The trees were stunted and prickly, the flowers were few and smelled of rotting meat and the only crops that would thrive were the famous Spink Valley onions, which grew to an enormous size but tasted so bitter they had to be boiled for four hours before even the goats would eat them.

Despite these trials, the McClouds enjoyed their early years in the valley. At the time, there were just three of them: Tim, Mary and little Peaches. Peaches was a happy child who spent her days playing about the farm, dressing up in her mother's clothes or drawing princesses – she was a precocious little girl – at the kitchen table. In the evening, Peaches would nestle between her parents on their threadbare sofa and her father would read her stories. They would hug her and kiss her and tell her that they were the luckiest parents in the world and that she was the most wonderful child that had ever lived.

Peaches could not have been happier.

But then one day, her mother announced that there would be a new arrival. A baby brother for Peaches to love. Peaches was confused. Were they not happy as they were? Was she not the most wonderful child that had ever lived? Why on earth would they want another one?

When little Indigo arrived, things turned out to be much worse than she had anticipated. He was small and pink and had a nasty wrinkled face just like a goblin. He squealed all the time and ate horrible mushy food and did smelly poos in his nappy. He was disgusting. Peaches could not understand why her parents actually seemed to like this dreadful little thing.

Worst of all, however, her mother no longer had time to play at dress-up, or sit with her drawing pictures of princesses. And in the evening, her father was so tired from getting up and tending to the baby in the night that he often fell asleep while reading her stories.

As Peaches watched her parents lavish attention on her hateful little brother, something small and dark blossomed in her heart. Each time her mother told her that she couldn't play with her just now, each time her father's head began to nod as he read her a story, that small dark something grew larger and darker. She thought about how wonderful life had been before Indigo arrived, and how wonderful it might be again if, for some reason, he was no longer around.

So it was that in his early years, Indigo McCloud gave his parents every impression of being remarkably accident-prone. On one occasion, he managed to glue himself to Ingrid the goat. Someone had left her stall open and he was found, stuck fast to the animal, many miles away. Another time, the vet was about to leave the family farm after treating Ingrid, who had become ill after eating most of the family's underwear as it dried on the washing line. He found Indigo wrapped up in sticky tape in the boot of his car. Another time, Indigo somehow ended up in a large cardboard box addressed to an orphanage just outside Mumbai in India.

The children's mother, Mary, though she loved her daughter dearly, could not help but wonder whether Peaches might actually be responsible for Indigo's misfortunes. She knew that it was quite common for first-born children to react badly to the arrival of a baby brother or sister, but Indigo continued to find himself in these perilous situations even after the arrival of Su and the twins.

The evening of the incident with the parcel and the orphanage, the children's mother lay in bed thinking that, from now on, she would keep a closer eye on her eldest daughter.

As for Tim McCloud, he never considered for one moment that Peaches might have caused these 'accidents'. As far as he was concerned, she was his darling little golden princess: gentle, kind, sensitive and thoughtful. As far as he was concerned, Peaches couldn't hurt a fly.

* * *

Indigo did not jolt suddenly awake. His return to consciousness was a slow business, filled with curious dreams and strange memories. He found himself cowering by the edge of a road as hundreds of porcelain toilets rained down upon him. Then the scene changed and he was being chased along the edge of the canal by a pack of Harmless dancing spiders. Then he was running across the roofs of Blunt. A giant Peaches – she must have been more than thirty metres tall – reached down, picked him up and dropped him into her pocket. Polly was hovering in the background constantly, calling to him.

Presently, the strange visions began to fade away, leaving only Polly, quietly calling his name in the same flat, emotionless tone of voice. Indigo blinked and tried to focus on the large glasses and the dangling pigtails slowly swimming into focus overhead. 'Polly ... what am I ... what ... ?'

Indigo sat up and felt a stabbing pain in his neck. He grunted and touched the spot – now quite swollen – where the spider had bitten him. He gingerly looked around, taking in the curtain, the bed, the hum of voices and the rattle of a trolley being pushed down a hall. He was in hospital. Now his eyes flew open and he turned to Polly, who sat with her hands in her lap, her eyes wide. She was rocking gently back and forth.

'Polly! You left your room.'

Polly didn't respond but remained staring and rocking.

'What happened?' Indigo asked.

'When the headset failed, I came down to the canal and found you lying in the vegetation. I called an ambulance.'

Indigo pushed himself upright and pivoted so that his legs dangled over the side of the bed. Another stabbing pain struck his leg. He winced, but didn't take his eyes from Polly. 'You came to get me.'

'Yes, Indigo.'

'Are you OK?'

Polly continued to rock quietly. 'I would like to go home as soon as possible.'

'Come on, then.' Indigo pushed himself from the edge of the bed and carefully lowered his left leg to the floor. It was still painful, but not intensely so.

'You have not yet seen a doctor, Indigo,' said Polly.

'Forget that. Polly?'

'Yes, Indigo.'

'When was the last time you left your house?'

Polly answered promptly. 'Four years, forty-eight days and thirty-six minutes ago.'

Indigo looked at his friend and for a moment forgot the pains in his neck and leg. He would have reached out and touched her except that Polly did not like to be touched.

'I can't believe you did that, Polly,' said Indigo. 'Thank you.'

Sitting up made Indigo feel woozy. The pain rose and fell like waves coming in and going out. He couldn't tell which felt stiffer – his neck or his leg.

A doctor strode past, talking loudly. Polly started. The rocking back and forth sped up slightly.

'It's OK, Polly. It's OK. You're going to be fine. We'll get you home now. Come on.'

Polly didn't move. Instead, she stared hard at Indigo, her eyes as wide as ever.

Indigo frowned. 'There's something else, isn't there? Is it Mandy? She's OK, right?'

'Yes.'

'There's something else wrong, though, isn't there?'

'Oswald Tripe has disappeared.'

9

The Funny Little Mind of Chief Inspector Milkweed

The town of Blunt has never had any shortage of eccentrics.

Bamber Adelyne, who made his millions in the sludge business, ate nothing but fig sandwiches and had all of the trees on his estate cut down because they reminded him too much of broccoli.

Elsbeth Quisk lived in a submarine moored on the River Blunt. She had been a world-renowned wig-maker, but it turned out that she'd got the hair for her wigs by kidnapping people, holding them prisoner on the submarine and shaving their heads. She escaped while awaiting trial and had never been seen again.

Erbolt Gweeb, the owner of the breadcrumb factory, had an enormous collection of clown costumes. He was also an exceptionally suspicious man. When he heard about Lucy Jones and her ordeal, he immediately decided that the incident was some sort of attempt to steal the Gweeb breadcrumb recipe, which had been in the family for generations and was the source of its fabulous wealth.

When he found out that Blunt's most senior police officer, Chief Inspector Milkweed, had been present at the scene and had allowed the thief to escape, he flew into a rage and came barging into Milkweed's office, demanding that he do something about it. Being a rich man, Gweeb was also a powerful man, with many even more powerful friends among Milkweed's superiors. Gweeb threatened to destroy the chief inspector's career if he did not catch the would-be breadcrumb-recipe thief – and fast!

Of course, every police officer in Blunt Police Station had heard Gweeb's shouted complaints and threats. In the week that followed, Milkweed's embarrassment about the whole business became more and more difficult to bear. He was sure that his junior officers were whispering and tittering about him behind his back.

How that made his blood boil!

He sat at his large desk in the police station, grinding his teeth and muttering to himself about breadcrumbs and geese and nasty boys who break into factories with large yellow diggers. Sometimes, Milkweed's muttering became so loud that his secretary, Ferguson, would stick his head around the door.

'Were you looking for me, sir?' he would ask.

'No!'

'Sorry, sir.'

Despite being a big man with long legs, fat fingers and a very large head, Milkweed had small features, which were clustered together at the centre of his face. When he became angry, he would forget to breathe in, so that his red face would slowly turn a rich, veiny purple, and his large head would quiver on his neck like a tuning fork. He also had the habit of clenching his fists involuntarily, so that whatever he was holding would suffer the consequences. So far that week, he had accidentally squashed his glasses, a pen-holder made out of a toilet roll insert that his niece Olive had given him and a large, ripe tomato. The juice of the tomato had gone everywhere, and he had to get Ferguson to take his uniform to the dry cleaner's while he sat in his underwear behind the desk, simmering with rage and trying not to squash anything else.

The longer Milkweed sat at his desk thinking about how the Breadcrumb Bandit (which is what he had started to call Indigo) had made a fool of him, the more he became convinced that the bandit also had something to do with the other unsolved crimes in Blunt.

Like the theft at Lexcorp, for example. Someone had blasted a hole in the wall and made off with a bank of computers. In Hosset's Scrummy Sweet Depot over on the east side of town, huge quantities of Bobbity Bars and cans of SugarCool had gone missing, together with two vending machines. Then there was that large pink and white armchair that disappeared from the window display in Williams's Furniture Store.

That morning, Milkweed had sent a team back to the factory to search for clues. If he caught the bandit – oh, what a sweet day that would be! Chief Inspector Milkweed sat back in his swivel chair and began to do the thing that he spent most of his day doing. Daydreaming.

His career to date had not been a glittering success. In addition to all those unsolved robberies, he had also mishandled the infamous sludge riots of '06. What a mess that had been! And it was Milkweed too who had been in charge when the disgraced wig-maker and notorious kidnapper Elsbeth Quisk had escaped some years earlier – a fact that had almost cost him his job. He managed to hold onto it for the same reason he got it in the first place: no-one else wanted to be chief inspector in Blunt.

But if he caught the bandit, why, that would make up for all the bad things that had gone before. If he caught the bandit, that would make him an excellent policeman in the eyes of his colleagues and his superiors. What a fine thing that would be!

Lost in this delightful fantasy, Milkweed imagined his superiors telephoning their congratulations. He imagined himself at the annual Chief Superintendent's Ball, holding his head up high and *not* overhearing people talking about 'that fool Milkweed' in the toilets. As for the Breadcrumb Bandit himself? Milkweed's eyes shone with malicious anticipation. Why, he would make sure that the hateful little villain felt the full weight of the law.

The chief inspector was pulled rudely from his daydream by a buzz from the intercom.

'Sorry, sir,' said Ferguson. 'There's a young girl out here, insists on seeing you.'

'A young girl? About what?'

'She wishes to report a crime, sir.'

'So let her tell you!' he shouted. 'That's your job, isn't it?'

'She insists on talking to you, sir.'

'Why?'

'She says it's very serious, sir.'

Milkweed sighed heavily. 'Oh, send her in, then. If you want anything done around here, you have to do it yourself.'

The door opened and in walked Mandy Tripe.

The previous day, after Indigo had saved her from the Harmless dancing spiders and she had managed to prise the traffic cone from her head, she had made her way back to town alone. Her majorette costume had been ruined by the sludge, but apart from that, she was more or less unhurt by her ordeal. She was, however, thoroughly bewildered by it. She had no idea what had happened to her or why. It was hard to believe that it could have been an accident, and almost as hard to believe that it wasn't.

But that evening, when her brother failed to return home, she began to suspect that the two incidents might somehow be connected. The visit of Peaches and her sisters had left a lasting impression on Mandy, and as the evening wore on and there was still no sign of Oswald, she became convinced that the McCloud girls had taken him.

Mandy considered bringing her suspicions to her parents. As she sat in her little bedroom, cracking her knuckles, she rehearsed the long, complicated explanation she would have to give and imagined the bemusement and disbelief that would follow it.

Peaches? Kidnap Oswald? Don't be daft, Mandy!

Though the Tripes had been living on Adenoid Terrace for less than two weeks, Peaches had already ingratiated herself with Mandy and Oswald's parents. The day after Oswald had dumped the pot of porridge on her head, Peaches had popped into their shop, Porridge Plus!, chatted with them for half an hour, then bought a large quantity of organic, gluten-free, free-range oatmeal for her father. At the time, Mandy had not understood the reason for the visit. Now, she began to see that Peaches had made it solely to leave a favourable impression on her mother and father.

This is why she decided to go straight to the police herself.

'It's my brother Oswald,' she said, holding her arms stiffly by her sides so she wouldn't start cracking her knuckles. 'He never came home last night. He ... he's been kidnapped.'

The chief inspector smiled warmly and held up his large, fat-fingered hand in a calming gesture.

'There, there, my dear, don't upset yourself,' he said. 'I'm sure your brother has just popped over to a friend's house. No doubt he'll be back for tea.'

'He's not at a friend's house,' said Mandy firmly. 'I checked with them all. He's been kidnapped. And I know who did it.'

Milkweed raised his eyebrows. 'Do you now?' he said.

Mandy drew herself up to her full height and raised her head of chestnut curls defiantly.

'Her name,' said Mandy, 'is Peaches McCloud. She lives at Number 21, Adenoid Terrace. She kidnapped him, I'm certain. Peaches and her sisters.'

'Peaches McCloud?' Chief Inspector Milkweed's little eyes widened. 'Adenoid Terrace? But we know Peaches well! She pops in every other week with a tray of something delicious for myself and my junior officers. Why, the child is a delight!' Milkweed hit a button on the intercom. 'Ferguson, what was it Peaches brought us in last week?'

'Cake pops, sir,' said Ferguson.

'Oh, yes! So tasty!'

'Yes, sir.'

Mandy quickly saw that the situation was swimming away from her. 'It's not just Oswald,' she blurted out. 'Yesterday, she ... there was a traffic cone and ... and there was this barge with sludge on it ... I ... I know she did something, I just know she did! And she came to my house, and ... and threatened me! She said that if I didn't sell –'

'Oh, come now, my dear.' Milkweed rose and came around to Mandy's side of the desk, smiling broadly. 'I think you've let your imagination run away with you.' The intercom buzzed again. 'What is it now, Ferguson?'

'The team are back from the breadcrumb factory, sir, and they've found something.'

'What? Send them in! Send them in!'

Mandy was instantly forgotten. Milkweed lumbered back to his side of the desk, sat down and began tapping his fingertips together, his eyes on the door.

'What about my brother?' Mandy asked.

Milkweed scowled at her. 'Oh ... talk to Ferguson, file a report ... whatever. Now, please, I have vital police business to attend to!'

Mandy stood a moment longer, staring at the small red features of the chief inspector, all of which were pointed at the door. She sighed heavily, turned and opened it – to two men in brown overalls. As she left, she heard Milkweed's voice booming behind her.

'Well, what did you find?'

One of the men opened up the dark leather satchel he carried and produced a small thin plastic bag with a torn scrap of black material inside.

'What's that?' said Milkweed

'We found it snagged on the digger that the perpetrator stole.'

'You mean the bandit?' Milkweed's eyes lit up. 'The Breadcrumb Bandit? It's from his clothing?'

The two men looked at each other. 'The what?'

'Never mind,' said Milkweed. 'What you're telling me is that this belongs to the one who tried to steal the bread-crumb recipe?'

'Well, yes, possibly, sir.'

Milkweed clapped his hands together in delight. 'Wonder-ful. You may go, gentlemen.' Milkweed hit a button on the intercom. 'Ferguson! We have him. Get the dog handlers in here! Now!'

'Yes, sir.'

Milkweed peered at the piece of material in the small plastic bag. 'I have you now, son, I have you now!'

10

The Reckless Return
to the Secret Chamber

In Polly's bedroom, Oswald's face filled the screen. Curly-headed like his sister, he wore a look of shock, as if someone had burst a balloon behind him just as the photograph was taken.

'OK, Polly,' said Indigo, 'tell me what you know.'

'He is tall, like his sister,' said Polly, '1.637 metres. He eats ice-cream cones from the bottom up. There is a rumour he sleepwalks, but it is not true. His left foot is slightly larger than his right foot. He plays skidball and is substitute puddle-keeper on the Blunt under-thirteens. He does not believe in the Eiffel Tower and never goes to the toilet on Wednesdays. His second favourite colour is greeny blue and his favourite breakfast is Dr Furry's Hamster Yumyums, which he ate accidentally last March and liked so much that he buys them secretly and keeps them under his bed.'

'What does he fear, Polly?' Indigo asked. 'What's the one thing he can't bear? For Lucy it was birds, and for Mandy it was spiders. What about snakes? Or wolves or, I don't know ... sharks?'

Polly hit a button on her screen and scrolled down. 'He doesn't like it when bits of pork chop get stuck in his teeth, and he hates the smell of mango chutney.'

Indigo was sitting on a chair in Polly's room, rubbing his still swollen neck, his leg stuck out straight in front of him. The crutch he had borrowed from the hospital to help him walk had been left outside the bedroom door because it was silver coloured and not the burnt umber that Polly preferred.

The return from the hospital had not been easy. Indigo would like to have waited until dark and kept to the back streets, but by the time they'd left, the distress of being away from the room in which she had remained for so long was almost too much for Polly to bear. She walked through the streets like a zombie, her eyes wide and unblinking behind her large glasses, while Indigo hobbled along behind her, trying to look in all directions at once. It was a windy evening in Blunt, which meant that the smoke from the Christmas-tree factory went swirling through the town, making weird smoky shapes dance down the streets. It was unnerving. Indigo kept thinking that he saw Su, Root and Berry, and sometimes even Peaches, walking towards them.

'This one is different,' said Indigo. 'With Mandy, Peaches just set it up to look like an accident. The girls set the ball rolling and walked away. This time someone actually grabbed Oswald and now they've imprisoned him somewhere.'

Polly's fingers danced on the keyboard. 'There are four hundred and twenty-seven empty premises in Blunt. The first one is the Crappy Tower Interpretive Centre. The second one is the old bingo hall, Goodtime Danny's, on Beetroot Street –'

'Polly –'

'The third one is the back room of the Nervy Clam on –'

'Polly, Polly. There's only one place to start. And we both know it.'

He limped to the window and stared out. Across the street, Lucy Jones's curtain twitched, and he saw briefly her pale, unsmiling face and her staring eyes. Guilt poked him in the ribs. He might have saved Mandy from the spiders, but Peaches had stolen Oswald from under his nose. Indigo had promised to protect the children of Adenoid Terrace, but he had failed.

'I'm going to have to go back to Peaches's underground HQ.'

Polly did not respond immediately but stared at her friend, then spun back to the computer and again the screen was filled with a series of complicated calculations.

'If you do that,' she said, 'your chances of getting caught are 62 per cent, rising to 81 per cent if you make the attempt on a Tuesday.'

Indigo shrugged. 'Got any better ideas?'

The difficulty with returning to the girls' underground HQ was that all four of his sisters were rarely out at the same time, even during school hours. If Peaches wished to miss a class, she would present the teacher with a note, which appeared to be signed by her dad or the school nurse or some other person in authority.

However, two days after Ingratitude Day, the bi-monthly Blunt and District girl scouts get-together was to be held in

Blunt Scouts Den. It was during this meeting that the girls would receive an update on how many calendars had been sold and who was leading the race for the new bicycle. This would be a big moment for Peaches, and one that neither she nor any of her sisters would miss.

That evening, Indigo sat on his bed, fiddling distractedly with the small red sports car that usually sat among the tattered paperbacks on his shelf, listening to the muffled scrapes, creaks, chatter and bickering which signified that his sisters were preparing to go out. Presently, he heard their door open and all four McCloud sisters tramped down the stairs and out the door.

Meanwhile, standing behind the net curtain in her room in Number 34, Polly Mole watched as they walked past wearing their brown and black girl-scout uniforms. Peaches strode in front, her head held high, smiling and waving to neighbours as she passed. Su padded silently behind her, while Root and Berry brought up the rear. Root was trying to stand on her twin's heels, while Berry was doing her best to elbow her sister in the stomach.

After Indigo's headset had broken down at Auntie Maggie's Big Hairy Spider Emporium, Polly replaced it with a much smaller one that sat securely inside Indigo's ear and was so comfortable that he could hardly feel it.

As soon as the girls turned left at the end of Adenoid Terrace, Indigo heard Polly's voice in the earpiece.

'Your sisters have cleared the terrace and are proceeding in a south-westerly direction along Brain Street, at an estimated speed of 1.78 metres per second.'

Indigo got stiffly to his feet and was about to cross the landing into his sisters' room when he heard his father's feet flip-flop up the stairs. They paused on the landing, then the door of his sisters' room creaked open and Indigo heard the clatter of his father's tool box being dropped onto the wooden floor. Indigo groaned in frustration. His father was trying to fix something. Indigo took out his new earpiece, got up and went across to the girls' room. Tim McCloud was kneeling at Su's bed and was about to take a large old-fashioned hand-drill to the leg.

'You OK, Dad?' Indigo asked.

His father sat back and pulled apart the long hair in front of his face as if it were a pair of grey curtains. 'Hiho, Indy! Just fixing Su's bed while she's out.'

'Need some help?'

'Great! Thanks, Indigo.'

Awakening Su in the morning was a hazardous exercise. Berry was usually awake first and would creep about the room, silently rousing Peaches and Root. All three would then place themselves outside the door of the bedroom and, at Peaches's signal, would roar in unison. 'TSUNAMI!'

Su was such a deep sleeper that this was the only way to wake her. The downside was that her first reaction was to strike out viciously with a devastating combination of kicks and chops. Her bed had so often been patched with bits of old timber, lengths of wire and steel bands, it looked as though it had been built entirely from scrap.

It took Indigo and his dad half an hour to repair the disintegrating bed. As Tim gathered up his tools and scraps of waste metal, Indigo glanced at his watch. The girl-scout get-togethers always lasted an hour, so that still gave him enough time to investigate the girls' HQ.

Unfortunately, however, as Tim McCloud turned and headed back downstairs, the girls had already emerged from the scout den and were walking down Adenoid Terrace towards home. Polly was standing rigidly at her window, talking rapidly into her headset: 'Indigo, come in Indigo. Your sisters' return is imminent. Repeat. Your sisters' return is imminent. Peaches, Tsunami, Root and Berry will be home within the next seventy-seven seconds.'

Indigo, however, had left his earpiece on the bed in his room. Polly's voice drifted unheard into the empty air.

Had Polly been good at spotting such things, she might have noticed that Peaches, as she strode down the terrace, was having trouble keeping the smile she always wore on her face. She might also have noted that all four girls were walking more quickly than usual and that the three younger ones seemed unduly nervous. Polly, however, was entirely taken up with the fact that Indigo was not responding to her repeated warnings.

As soon as Tim McCloud returned downstairs, Indigo reached under Berry's bed and pulled the lever; the dressing table swung across and the door opened. He descended quickly to Peaches's HQ.

There was no sign of Oswald.

Everything, in fact, was almost exactly the same as before. The room was large, white, quiet and softly lit. The computers, the workbench, the vending machines, chairs and couch were just as they had been. The whiteboard, however, was completely blank. Only the peach-scented hit list remained, and as before, only Lucy's name had been crossed out.

Moving quickly, Indigo circled the room, opening drawers and cupboards, checking under tables and chairs, but found nothing. He sighed heavily and sat down in Peaches's large pink and white armchair. There was something hard underneath him. Reaching under the seat, he pulled out a copy of *Kittens in Bonnets & Bunnies in Cardigans*. It was the bumper spring edition.

Suddenly there were footsteps overhead. Indigo shoved the book back under the seat and limped for the stairs. As he reached the girls' room, he could hear the clatter of many feet making their way up the house stairs. From the kitchen below, his father called out. 'Hiho, Su! Fixed your bed!'

Peaches swung the door open and stomped in. Her face was a mask of black fury. She spun round and faced the girls, her fists clenched, her eyes blazing.

'How could this happen? How could it?'

'Five hundred and three calendars have been sold on your account so far, Peaches,' said Root nervously. 'We didn't think anyone else would get close.'

'We've got time to catch up,' said Berry. 'We'll sell loads more.'

Standing before their eldest sister in their black and brown uniforms, Root, Berry and Su appeared like a squadron of soldiers who had done something to displease their commanding officer. Root was grinding her misshapen teeth, Berry's dark eyes were darting about nervously, while Su was blinking rapidly, chewing on her lower lip.

'That girl made a fool of me! Of me! Peaches McCloud! In front of the whole town! How could this happen?'

'We'll deal with her, Peaches.' The twins spoke together. 'Just as soon as her kid brother is sorted out,' Berry added. 'The Bad Claw will get him by lunchtime on Saturday, then he'll know what it's like to –'

Suddenly, Peaches stiffened. Berry instantly fell silent.

'Do you feel that?' asked Peaches quietly.

No-one spoke.

Peaches spun round. The window, which looked out on the McClouds' tiny back yard, was ever-so-slightly open. If there was one thing Peaches McCloud couldn't stand, it was an open window in her bedroom. She spoke quietly and slowly. 'Did one of you open this window?'

Su shook her head rapidly.

'Her!' said Root and Berry together, pointing at each other.

'No, it wasn't,' said Root. 'It was her!'

'I never!' said Berry. 'She –'

Peaches held a finger in the air to silence them. Then she marched to the window and opened it fully. Leaning out, she inspected the yard below, then held her breath and listened. The distant braying of the donkeys could be heard through the smoky evening air, mingling with the B flat minor scale playing repeatedly in the accordion factory. Directly above her head, Indigo clung to the gutter, desperately trying to keep his throbbing leg from slipping. If she looked up, she would see him.

Peaches remained perfectly still for what felt like an incredibly long time, then slowly drew her head inside the window and pulled it closed.

11

The Terrible Fate
of Mary McCloud

The following morning, Adenoid Terrace buzzed with the news that Mandy Tripe had sold eighty-nine more calendars than Peaches McCloud.

The Tripes, it turned out, had a very large extended family in the neighbouring towns of Bulstrode and Cragmire. This family was exceptionally closely knit. Whenever any member was in trouble or needed help, the rest of the clan would rally round. Mandy and Oswald had a total of twenty-seven first cousins. All had taken to the streets of their towns and sold vast numbers of souvenir calendars on Mandy's behalf.

For the first time that anyone could remember, someone had got one up on Peaches McCloud.

All of this calendar selling had, of course, happened before Oswald's disappearance. When he failed to come home the night after the Ingratitude Day parade, Mandy had very quickly forgotten all about souvenir calendars, girl scouts and bikes. Though she failed to convince Chief Inspector Milkweed that Peaches had anything to do with her brother's disappearance, she did file a missing persons report with Ferguson. Soon after that, two policemen arrived out to Number 43, Adenoid Terrace, where the Tripes lived, in order to ask questions and take notes. They were admitted to the house by Bill Tripe, Mandy and Oswald's father. He was a tall, sharp-elbowed man whose curly hair rimmed the bald dome of his head. His wife, Leonora, was a short, energetic woman who wore her curls piled on top of her head like a collection of birds' nests. While the policemen asked their questions, she sat on the couch, dabbing at her eyes with a yellow hankie.

'I just want my boy back home with me!' she wailed.

Mr Tripe put his arm around her shoulder. 'Just get him back for us, officers, please.'

Mandy watched the two policemen carefully. They were both quite young. One of them was a little shorter than Mandy. His voice was so unnaturally high that, for a while, Mandy thought he was putting it on. She had scowled at him until she realised that that was just the way he spoke. The other one was, she thought, far too jolly. He had a fat face with quite an impressive moustache that could not cover the broad grin underneath. It was as if he had heard a joke just before he left the station and it kept popping back into his head.

They were, however, very diligent and asked many questions about the last time Oswald had been seen and about his friends and his habits. When they had finished, Mandy followed them to the door. Making sure that her parents were out of earshot, she asked quietly, 'What do you think happened to him? Really.'

The two policemen stood on the doorstep and glanced at each other.

'Well, miss,' said the jolly one, 'we do find in most of these cases that the young people turn up safely in the end.' He flicked back through the notebook in his hand. 'He's been working night and day in your parents' shop. I'm pretty sure he just got a little tired of it and decided to take a holiday.'

'Yes, that seems most likely,' said the second policeman.

Mandy looked from one to the other in alarm. 'No! That's not it at all. I know him well – he would never do that, never!'

At that moment, activity further down the street prompted the shorter policeman to glance around. His eyes lit up. 'Why, it's Peaches McCloud!' he squeaked.

The other policeman turned to look. 'Ha ha!' he cried. 'So it is!' He pocketed his notebook and followed his colleague out onto the street. 'Hello, Peaches!' he called.

Mandy watched them in disbelief. 'But … but, what about Oswald?'

'Why, Officers Burke and Hare!' Peaches called, coming towards them. 'Fancy seeing you here!'

She was wearing a royal blue silk chiffon dress, her hair braided into a single plait, which she wore swept forward over one shoulder. Her smile had returned; there was no trace of the tension that Polly hadn't noticed the previous evening. Peaches saw Mandy, and her smile broadened. 'Oh, Mandy, it's you! Congratulations on your calendar selling! I'm delighted you're doing so well!'

Mandy ignored her. 'My brother,' she said forcefully, trying to reclaim the policemen's attention. 'I don't think you –'

'Thanks for those cake pops last week, Peaches,' said the short policeman. 'They were yummilicious!'

'Oh, yes!' said the jolly one, rubbing his tummy.

'Don't mention it at all, please,' said Peaches. 'It's just my way of acknowledging the wonderful work that you do. And I do hope you like caramel squares!' She glanced at Mandy as she said this.

'My favourite!' squeaked the first policeman.

Peaches winked. 'You're in for a treat next Friday so, Officer Burke.' But now she raised a hand to her throat and wrinkled her delicate brow. 'Oh, my gosh, but if you're here, officers, something must be wrong. I do hope nothing unpleasant has happened?'

'Oh, it's just young Oswald Tripe,' said the jolly policeman with what Mandy thought was a dismissive wave of his hand. 'He's just taken a little holiday from Mum and Dad. Working him too hard, don't you know.'

Mandy tried once again to interject but was drowned out by Peaches's gasp of horror. 'Oh, poor Mandy! How worried you must be. I don't know what I'd do if anything happened to my little brother. Do tell me if there's anything at all I can do, won't you? Officers, you must do everything in your power to find Oswald. I do hope nothing *beastly* has happened to him!'

Mandy was sure that she was the only one to hear the curious emphasis on the word 'beastly'.

* * *

When Indigo McCloud was five years old, the peaceful country life that the family had been enjoying in the Spink Valley came to an end when construction began on a six-lane motorway linking the towns of Bulstrode and Cragmire. The original plans for this road brought it through the Spivvet Marshes, which lay a couple of kilometres from the farm on which the family lived. These plans had to change, however, when ecologists discovered one of the country's last remaining habitats for scabby weed – a rubbery plant with a yellow flower that smelled of vomit – on the marsh. As a result, the road had to divert around it. The new route came right through the middle of the farm. In order to milk the cow or feed the goat, it became necessary to cross all six lanes of the new motorway, while the roar of traffic kept everyone awake half the night.

One day, not long after the motorway had opened, Mary and little Indigo were crossing the road to collect eggs from the henhouse, when a large articulated lorry piled high with toilets pulled in to ask directions. The lorry driver explained that the toilets were bound for the new prison in Blunt, but he had – he thought – taken the wrong exit leaving Bulstrode. Indigo's mother, shouting over the roar of the traffic, gave the driver the correct route. He thanked her and pulled away, and as he did, the load of toilets, which had been very poorly stacked, came loose. Mary McCloud, her attention on Indigo, did not notice what was happening until it was almost too late. She heard the crash as the first toilet toppled from the load. Spinning around, she seized Indigo by the shoulders and flung him to safety. Indigo landed on all fours in the weeds and grass that grew along the verge, then looked up to see all one hundred and eleven toilets come crashing down upon his mother in a horrendous avalanche of porcelain.

When Indigo was found wandering along the edge of the road, dazed and confused, an hour later, his hair had turned completely grey.

Afterwards, a grief-stricken Tim McCloud decided that he could no longer remain in the Spink Valley and moved his family to Blunt, specifically to Adenoid Terrace.

'The Incident', which it quickly came to be known as in the family, seemed only to nourish the dark flower that had blossomed in Peaches's heart shortly after Indigo's arrival. As the days went by, her view of life became increasingly dark and horribly twisted. The world became a bitter place, where chaos ruled, where a wonderful life could be ripped away from you to leave you stranded on a miserable street in a miserable town, surrounded by idiots and weaklings. For Peaches, the only way to survive in such a terrible place was to take whatever you wanted from whomever you wanted, and to pretend that you were one thing in order for you to be something else entirely.

So, she gave up trying to get rid of Indigo and instead turned her attention to her younger sisters, not with the intention of trying to get rid of them too, but rather of moulding them into children who would see the world the way Peaches saw it and do whatever it was that Peaches wanted. She was exceptionally successful in this regard.

While Indigo managed to stay alive, the horrifying nature of what had happened to him left an indelible mark. He became a suspicious, solitary boy, who avoided the company of others. Terrified that Peaches might turn her wrath on him once again, Indigo made sure to do nothing to draw attention to himself. He moved about his life – as Lucy Jones had suggested – like a mouse: barely noticeable, hardly there at all. He kept to his room with its milk-crate furniture and threadbare carpet, where he reread his books and stared out the window and dreamed of what life might have been like if The Incident had never happened.

It was a boring existence, or would have been if he had not discovered the roofs and how well they interconnected, how it was possible, with a little practice, to cross from one end of the town to the other without ever setting foot on the ground. Up on the roofs, Indigo had an entire world to explore. He found that people hardly ever looked up and that it was possible to move above them without discovery. Alone on the roofs, he became highly skilled at the range of balances, jumps, somersaults and flips that one needs to cross a roofscape quickly and without accident.

It was up on the roofs that Indigo felt alive. There, the real Indy emerged from the shell of the scared little boy that lived on the street below.

Being a small boy with grey hair is not easy. Being a small boy with grey hair in a new town is even less so. Every new child that Indigo met on Adenoid Terrace had something to say about the strangeness of his appearance. They called him 'Grandpa' and tugged at his hair to see if it was a wig.

One girl, however, did not do any of these things.

Even as a very little girl, Polly Mole wore large-framed glasses and parted her hair exactly down the middle, dividing it into perfectly symmetrical pigtails. She walked up to Indy and said, 'There are more than one hundred breeds of domestic duck.'

'Really?'

'Yes,' said Polly. 'They don't actually quack that much. They chirp and grunt far more often.'

Indigo, happy to be engaged in a conversation that did not involve his hair, thought for a minute and then said, 'You probably know a lot of things about ducks.'

'Yes,' said Polly, 'I do.' She paused. 'My mother says I mustn't bore people about ducks. She said first to ask if you want to hear about ducks.'

'I want to hear about ducks.'

And so Polly continued to talk about ducks for perhaps fifteen minutes, before Indigo invited her into his house to play.

12

The Frantic Search for Oswald Tripe

'The Bad Claw will get him by lunchtime Saturday, then he'll know what it's like to …'

For perhaps the fiftieth time since they had begun their investigations, Indigo repeated the line he had heard Berry say while he clung to the gutter outside his sisters' bedroom. He was pacing up and down behind Polly's chair. His leg, though it continued to ache dully, had lost its stiffness and now at least he was able to move freely. In the intervening time, however, he had hardly left Polly's bedroom. There, he and Polly had worked tirelessly, trying to figure out what the Bad Claw might be. They had considered every clawed animal they could think of, from bears to otters to armadillos, but there was no way to connect any of these beasts with a threat to Oswald Tripe.

'There's something I'm missing,' said Indigo, slapping his fist into his palm.

'Lobsters have been known to grow as large as 12 kilos,' said Polly. 'Oswald weighs 49.8 kilos, however. Therefore he should be able to fight off a giant lobster with ease, unless it was armed or had undergone special training.'

Indigo shook his head. 'Oswald's crime had nothing to do with selling calendars, right? He dumped a load of smelly porridge over Peaches. So maybe the punishment is going to fit the crime. Maybe the rest of the sentence was something like, "He'll know what it's like to have his hair smell bad …"'

'Bad-smelling hair,' said Polly slowly. 'Is that terrible?'

Indigo returned to the window and stared across at Lucy's house. He had called to see her earlier that day, and once again Lucy's parents had told him that she remained in a state of shock, tormented by visions of savage geese, and could not have visitors. As he looked out into the street, two unfamiliar curly-haired girls arrived at Number 43, the Tripes' house, and knocked. Indigo watched Mandy admit them and close the door again.

'How many cousins exactly do Mandy and Oswald have?' Indigo asked.

'Twenty-seven,' said Polly. 'They intend to send out search parties to look for Oswald.'

Indigo, staring again at Lucy's window, shook his head. 'Search parties won't be enough. He'll be too well hidden. We need to figure out what she meant. We need to figure out what she's going to do to him.'

By Saturday morning, however, Indigo could think of nothing better than Polly's suggestion about lobsters, which is why he made his way over the roofs of Blunt to the warehouse district.

The morning was smoky and damp, without a puff of wind. The drizzle that had been falling for most of the week had now become a misty fog, which merged with the smoke to cut visibility down to almost nothing. Indigo moved carefully over the roofs, taking care to avoid the corrugated iron that covered so many of the buildings in this part of town. He found it impossible to move quietly across iron, and in the rain, it became treacherously slippery. Eventually, he came to the large warehouse in which Blunt's weekly fish market used to be held. He found a dusty, cobweb-choked window high in the wall and squeezed through, then climbed down the inner wall, finding footholds in the broken plaster and brickwork.

The building was vast and gloomy and, of course, smelled very strongly of fish. Indigo picked his way through the puddles of water that had accumulated on the concrete floor, past the piles of fish crates stacked about the place. He searched for two hours before giving up.

'He's not here, Polly,' he said into his headset, angrily kicking a fish crate. The noise echoed loudly around the warehouse. 'We're on the wrong track.'

'I suggest you return to Adenoid Terrace.'

Indigo shook his head. 'No, it's today. Something awful is going to happen to Oswald within the next couple of hours. We've got to figure out what it is.'

He was back on the roof of the warehouse, making his way quietly along the concrete ridge at the edge of the building, when he glanced down and noticed two figures among the few people that moved about the streets below him. The fog and smoke made it difficult to see, but there was something about the way they moved that made Indigo pause and watch as they continued towards him, then turned right at the corner. As they turned, the one ray of sunlight that penetrated the smoke caught them for the briefest moment. Girls. One tall, one short.

'It's Root and Berry, Polly,' said Indigo. 'I can see Root and Berry.'

He ran lightly across the edge of the warehouse roof to the corner and saw the girls move purposefully down the street. Every now and again, Root, the smaller of the two, would glance behind and scan the path along which they had come. For the first time that Indigo could remember, both were silent. There was no bickering, no punching, no biting or elbowing.

Berry had something in her hand, something small. Indigo shadowed them as they reached the end of the building, but could not get close enough to identify the object. He crouched at the edge of the warehouse roof and watched them cross the river at the Crappy Tower, then disappear into the smog that completely shrouded the Eelfields beyond.

* * *

The Crappy Tower had been built from Spink Valley sandstone in 1974 as part of Blunt's unsuccessful bid to host the World Wellie-Throwing Games. It was supposed to look like a Wellington boot, but because Spink Valley sandstone is soft and unsuitable for building, it had been badly eroded by the wind, making it tall and knobbly. Over time, the smoke from the Christmas-tree factory deepened the tower's pale shade of brown, making it look more like a piece of poo with each passing year. The townspeople had campaigned to have it demolished, but the council could not afford to carry out the demolition safely. In the meantime, wind erosion had undermined the structure, making it dangerous. The base of the tower was surrounded by fences decorated with 'Keep Out' signs.

The Eelfields was a large grassy area inside a loop created by the river as it wound its way out of town. Many years earlier, hundreds of Blunt women worked there, gutting the eels that had been caught in the eel fisheries along the river and preparing them for sale in the big eel market in Cragmire. Unfortunately, however, shortly after the plastic-Christmas-tree factory opened, a black gooey substance leaked from the factory into the river, killing off everything except for a species of yellow eel so vicious that people were discouraged from swimming in the river in case they were attacked. These eels, which went on to thrive in the polluted water, were mostly bone, tasted terrible and in any case were poisonous.

Balanced at the edge of the warehouse roof, Indigo peered into the gloom but could not see any trace of the girls.

'I think they're … I think they're talking to someone. I think I can hear voices.'

'Perhaps they are fighting.'

'No, not this time.'

Indigo scanned the roof, looking for a quick way down, but that would require going back the way he had come and risk losing track of the girls. He hovered, squinting into the smoke, straining to pick up the faint voices emerging from it. Before long, the girls reappeared. Berry, Indigo noted, was no longer carrying the small package he had seen in her hand minutes before. He waited for them to pass up the street, with the intention of dashing towards the Eelfields to try to see who they had met, but as they returned across the river and passed the Crappy Tower, they did not turn for home.

'They're heading up Wriggle Street, Polly. Now what? Do I follow them or figure out where they just were?'

'The objective is to find Oswald Tripe, correct?'

'Of course.'

'The Eelfields lacks any kind of structure where they might imprison Oswald,' said Polly. 'Which makes it unlikely that he is there. I recommend you follow Root and Berry.'

The warehouse roof ended at an alleyway, so Indigo took a run, leaped and landed like a cat on the opposite roof. Wriggle Street was a jumble of shops and houses of varying shapes and sizes; he had to scamper up ledges and along the peaks of pitched roofs to keep up with his sisters. He leap-frogged chimneys, slid down drainpipes and leaped alleyways, always careful to keep them in view and to keep his movements as silent as possible.

Presently, the girls turned down an alleyway, then another that led from that. Peering down through the smoke, Indigo feared for a moment that he had lost them but, dashing along the roof of Erewok's Cut-Price Noodle House, he saw them pause at the mouth of Belly Lane and check in all directions.

Cheddar's Curry House stood next door to Erewok's. Indigo dashed to the edge of the roof and jumped down towards Cheddar's, but in his haste to ensure that he did not lose his sisters, he failed to register the fact that Cheddar's roof was unlike any of the others he had crossed that morning. In an effort to make his restaurant more exotic, Cheddar Williams had built an outdoor eating area in his back yard, complete with grass roof.

13

The Terrible Curries
of Cheddar Williams

As soon as Mandy Tripe realised that the police weren't going to be much help getting her brother back, she did just as she had done when she needed help selling calendars. She called her cousins. Each member of the Tripe family was always ready to drop everything and go to the aid of a Tripe in distress. When Uncle Charlie Tripe had his ice-cream van repossessed by the bank, for example, Mandy and Oswald spent three days with him sorting out his finances. Just before Granny Tripe was released from prison, all twenty-seven cousins descended on her house and repainted it, took out all the old carpets and replaced them with bright, clean lino. Most recently, when Little Molly Tripe broke her leg while rescuing a puppy from a well, Mandy and Oswald travelled to Cragmire every day to visit her in hospital.

Within hours of Mandy's distress call, the Tripe cousins began to arrive in Blunt. Hortense and Aurelia Tripe were the first to show up. The girls, who were eleven and twelve years old respectively, loved mystery novels and were both thrilled at the possibility of getting their teeth into a real-life mystery (though of course they were also horrified to learn of Oswald's disappearance). The triplets, Larry, Harry and Xanthipides were next. They lived on a farm and came laden down with vegetables, eggs, home-made bread and marmalade to feed the troops. Ichabod Tripe brought electronic trackers, night-vision goggles and a host of other spying equipment. Wolfgang and Trudy Tripe, whose parents kept a German sausage shop on Bulstrode High Street, showed up with a variety of preserved and spiced meats.

Though they came from all walks of life, the Tripe cousins had one thing in common. Every single one had thick chestnut-coloured curls.

Last to arrive was Little Molly Tripe, still wearing a cast from her accident with the puppy down the well. She had come all the way from Cragmire on the bus on her own. By the time she arrived, the house was jam-packed with Tripe cousins stuffing their faces with German sausage, boiled eggs and home-made brown bread and marmalade. They were all arguing loudly about the best way to find Oswald.

The living room fell silent and the crowds parted as Mandy led Little Molly in. Moving slowly and carefully, with a look of great concentration on her freckled face, Little Molly came hobbling into the room on crutches. Her huge cast – completely covered in signatures and tiny drawings – was almost as big as she was and her dome of bouncy curls was held back by a tartan headband. She looked up at her larger cousins through huge green eyes.

'I heard Oswald was in trouble,' she said, 'so I came as fast as I could.'

Cheddar's Curry House, the best-known restaurant in Blunt, was particularly famous for two things: the strength of Cheddar's curries and the effect they had on the digestive system. Cheddar's squid jalfrezi was so hot that few people had ever managed to get through an entire plate. And every person who ever consumed any one of Cheddar Williams's curries subsequently generated the most astonishingly smelly farts.

Indigo dropped through the grass roof of Cheddar's as if it were, well, made of grass, and made a terrific din as he landed amid a pile of cardboard boxes, plastic trays and rubbish bags. Sadly for Cheddar, Blunt's climate was so wet and the smoke so inescapable that his outdoor eating area had proved very unpopular. Now, instead of tables, chairs and hungry diners, the grass-roofed patio was full of rubbish.

Cheddar's kitchen was exceptionally busy that lunchtime. Chefs, waiters, porters and kitchen boys bustled about, while Cheddar himself stood in the middle of the chaos shouting orders and scratching at his short black beard with the edge of the very large meat cleaver he carried with him everywhere. Dressed in a white chef's uniform stained with various types of curry, Cheddar was enormously fat and exceptionally bad tempered. The slightest thing sent him into a rage. Because this was a particularly important lunchtime in the life of the restaurant, Cheddar was even more on edge than usual. He was roaring at a kitchen porter to breathe more quietly when an unexpected guest dropped into his back yard. He stopped what he was doing and came out to investigate the crash. When he saw a boy with grey hair picking himself up from the rubbish, he flew into a rage.

'Thief!' he roared, raising the meat cleaver high in the air. 'You are trying to steal from Cheddar!'

'No!' cried Indigo. 'I just –'

'Liar!' screamed Cheddar and came charging towards Indigo, the cleaver raised. Indigo got to his feet in the nick of time and deftly sidestepped the lumbering chef.

Polly's voice crackled over the headset. 'Is there a problem, Indigo?'

'A slight problem, Polly.'

'Would you like me to talk about ducks?'

'Maybe later, Polly.'

The little yard was completely enclosed, which meant that Indigo's only means of escape lay through the door through which Cheddar had just emerged. As the large cleaver-wielding restaurateur turned towards him, Indigo tore open the door and dashed into the kitchen.

'STOP HIM!' Cheddar roared.

The kitchen staff sprang into action at their boss's command. Kitchen boys dived for Indigo, porters grabbed at him, but Indigo, desperate not to lose his sisters and the possibility that they would lead him to Oswald, refused to allow himself to be caught. He ducked, rolled and skipped past each tackle. Something whizzed past his ear. He looked up as Cheddar's cleaver slammed into the door above him and stuck fast. Cheddar roared again and grabbed another cleaver from a knife-block on the counter as Indigo made it to the double doors and burst into the dining room.

Though he focused immediately on the exit into the street at the far end of this room, there were several details about it and its occupants which Indigo couldn't help but notice. For one thing, there were a great many of these occupants. For another, almost all of them were fat, some exceptionally so. They were wedged into benches and chairs and squeezed behind tables in a room that couldn't quite fit them all. That probably explained why none of them made any effort to stand up and intercept Indigo. As he scrambled between them, they tutted angrily and muttered things about bad manners and not being able to eat their curries in peace.

There was one other detail that Indigo noticed, just before he made it to the front door. This was the large banner hanging the length of the restaurant: 'Cheddar's Curry House Welcomes the Blunt and District Curry Lovers' Association (West)'.

Indigo pulled open the front door and dashed out into the smog, Cheddar and his staff in hot pursuit. But there was something Indigo had seen in the previous three seconds that set off a tiny alarm in his mind. In the rush to escape, it risked being entirely lost, but as he turned towards Belly Lane in the hope of shaking off his pursuers and finding out where Root and Berry had gone, the alarm became more insistent. *Blunt and District Curry Lovers' Association (West) ... Blunt and District Curry Lovers' Association (West) ...* B-A-D-C-L-A-(W) – BAD CLAW!

Indigo skidded to a halt and spun round just as Cheddar and assorted kitchen staff, armed with knives, frying pans, rolling pins and so on, burst out through the door. One porter, who didn't have the time to grab anything else, brandished an ice-cream scoop.

'What have you done with Oswald Tripe?' Indigo called.

'What?' said Cheddar, striding menacingly towards him, his cleaver poised to strike.

'Oswald Tripe!' said Indigo, standing his ground. 'You or someone in that restaurant knows where he is.'

'Oswald Tripe? Wait …' Absently handing his cleaver to one of his chefs, Cheddar reached into his back pocket and pulled out a piece of paper, which he unfolded. 'Oswald Tripe, you say?' He squinted at the paper. 'But this is the missing boy! His cousin was here earlier – she told me of his disappearance.' Now Cheddar's face grew dark and he snatched the cleaver from his underling. 'You think I had something to do with that?' he snarled. 'How dare you! I would never hurt a child!' He swung the cleaver at Indigo, who stepped backwards briskly. 'Now get out and never come back, or I will make thief curry!'

With that, Cheddar turned and strode back into his restaurant, followed by his entourage of glowering kitchen boys, porters and sub-chefs.

Indigo stood rooted to the spot, thinking hard. The BAD CLAW – they were just a bunch of curry lovers. How could they hurt Oswald? But it couldn't possibly be a coincidence, could it? That Root and Berry had led him here? And that the initials should spell out exactly that for which he and Polly had spent the last two days looking?

'Polly, the BAD CLAW is the Blunt and District Curry Lovers' Association (West). Find out all you can about it. And Cheddar's Curry House, everything you can find out about that too.'

As Polly searched, Indigo moved quietly towards Belly Lane, which ran down one side of the restaurant. It was here that he had last seen Root and Berry. The lane was deserted. He looked up at the large oblong building alongside the restaurant. It was the old portaloo factory, long since closed down.

'The BAD CLAW meets six times a year to eat curry,' said Polly.

'Go on.'

'It used to be called the Blunt and District Curry Lovers' Association, but there was a dispute about which rice should be served at their twenty-seventh annual gala dinner, steamed or fried. Afterwards, the group split into a west faction and an east faction. Its current president, Ian Snit, works as a traffic warden and once had all of his cardigan buttons bitten off by an angry motorist. His mother has a collection of tropical –'

'What about Cheddar's?' Indigo, short on time, cut across his friend. He was looking up at the large silver pipe that emerged from one side of the curry house and crossed the alley into the portaloo factory.

'Cheddar's Curry House was opened in 1984 by Gopal 'Cheddar' Williams, after he retired from the professional cheese-rolling circuit. A tax audit in 1985 –'

'Hang on, Polly.' Indigo stared up at the pipe. 'Has he done any work on the restaurant lately?'

'Yes. He installed a new air conditioning system four weeks ago. The Turbo AirCon 5500, the most powerful in the world. The logical conclusion is that the system was installed because his curries generate such awful farts.'

Indigo went still. 'That's it ... That's it.'

'That's what?'

Indigo ran to the wall of the old portaloo factory and began scaling the building. He leaped from window ledge to window ledge, hauling himself higher and higher until he reached the roof. Here, he paused, scanning the roofscape, then took off towards the small shed-like building that projected from its centre. Its door was unlocked.

He was right; he was sure he was right, but time was against him. If he didn't move fast, Oswald was done for.

Inside, the building was almost completely dark. Only the patchy daylight filtering in from narrow, widely spaced windows set high in the walls provided any illumination. Indigo gripped the steel banister as he made his way down the steps towards the ground floor. Aware that Root, Berry or any of his sisters might be lurking about, he tried to move as quietly as possible, but the building was so vast and so full of echoes, it was impossible to dampen the sound of his feet striking the steps on the iron staircase.

The floor of the factory was stacked with ancient portaloos, some of them rising forty or fifty feet above the ground. They created a maze of narrow, gloomy corridors that turned first one way, then the other, guiding Indigo deep into the factory. He paused at what sounded like a muffled groan somewhere up ahead. This was followed by a thumping noise. Indigo crept forward, his gaze focused upwards, until, rounding a bend, he saw the glint of a silver pipe, the same pipe that had emerged from Cheddar's. He followed it and saw that it terminated in a portaloo that was stacked high above him.

Indigo threw himself at the tower of portaloos and began climbing. He reached the portaloo in question in seconds, pulled the door open and gagged.

The smell was unlike anything he had ever smelled before. In the second it took him to clamp his fingers about his nose, it rushed into his nostrils, reached down into his stomach and squeezed. Indigo almost threw up. It was a kind of curry-flavoured awfulness so foul that its fumes turned the air a shade of luminous green. For one terrible moment, Indigo felt as if he was trapped in the stomach of a donkey who had died three weeks earlier from eating a vindaloo of rancid pork and rotten eggs.

Holding his breath, Indigo peered through the green fumes and started backwards in horror. There, half-propped against one side of the portaloo, was what appeared to be a huge squirming maggot. Grey and segmented, it writhed and wriggled in its narrow prison, moaning and thumping against the thin plastic wall. Indigo squinted at the head of the bizarre creature and saw what appeared to be a human nose. And there, just above it, a tuft of curly hair.

'Oswald!' Indigo cried, understanding now that the thing was not some kind of freakish monstrosity, but a human being, completely wrapped in grey tape.

So it was that Peaches's diabolical plan was laid bare.

As the members of the Blunt and District Curry Lovers' Association (West) worked their way through their curries, they did what every person who consumed Cheddar's curries did. They farted. They farted the most stomach-churning, eye-watering, nose-hair-singeing farts that anyone in the history of spicy food had ever produced. And as they did, Cheddar's high-powered ventilation system drew each and every one of those terrible farts from the restaurant and brought them directly to the portaloo in which Oswald was imprisoned. There, he alone suffered the onslaught of the dreadful smells, unable to move, unable to do anything but breathe through his nose.

Indigo pulled Oswald from his tiny prison and half-climbed, half-fell down onto the factory floor. Still holding his breath, he dragged the stricken Tripe all the way back to the foot of the steel stairs, ripped the tape from his face, then collapsed onto the ground, breathing heavily.

Oswald sucked in breath after breath of clean air.

'Sm … sm … smell,' he panted. 'The smell!'

'It's over, Oswald,' said Indigo. 'You're safe.'

It took Indigo more than half an hour to unwrap the tape which clung to Oswald. Shaking and weak from being confined in such a small space for so long, it took Oswald another half-hour to gather the strength to even stand up.

He had no idea what had happened to him.

One minute he was on his way to the Ingratitude Day parade to see his sister march, the next thing he woke up in the dark unable to move. Then, about half an hour before

Indigo showed up, the air in the portaloo had become steadily worse.

As he pulled the last bits of tape from his clothes and hair, Oswald shook his head. 'Dunno what would've happened if you hadn't come along.' He shuddered and gagged again at the memory of the stink.

'Hang on,' said Indigo, squinting at Oswald's hair. 'What's that?'

'What?' said Oswald. He touched the back of his head and his hand instantly recoiled. Gingerly, he felt it again.

'It's … it's a bald spot!' Oswald winced. 'Someone shaved a bit of my hair. Why would anyone do that?'

By the time they emerged from the factory, the feeling had returned to Oswald's legs and he could walk unaided.

'Do me a favour,' said Indigo. 'Don't tell anyone it was me who let you out. Just tell them you escaped.'

'OK, Indigo. I owe you one.'

The two boys parted outside the factory. Indigo took to the roofs, feeling as good as he could ever remember feeling. Together, he and Polly had saved Mandy, they had saved Oswald, they had come out of the shadows, they had shrugged off their fear and done something good. Something real and good. Indigo paused on the roof of a house in Adenoid Terrace and looked out over the town, savouring a warmth that he had not known before. At Number 21, he slid down the tiles, swung in through the window and landed in his room.

Someone was waiting for him.

14

The Fiendish Scheming
of Peaches McCloud

'Hi, Indy,' said Peaches brightly. 'How are you?'

Indigo froze. His mind went blank; it was as if someone had suddenly pulled out his plug, leaving him standing there like a piece of useless equipment. That wonderful feeling, that warmth in his chest, disappeared so quickly it was as if it had never existed.

Peaches was wearing a pair of designer jogging pants and a matching hoodie in canary yellow and was leaning against the door with her head cocked at an angle, her thick locks bunched up around her chin.

'You were out early this morning, Indigo,' she said, inspecting her nails, which were the same shade of yellow. 'And fancy you not using the door. How very peculiar!'

Though his body remained utterly immobile, Indigo's mind started to power back up. It could only, however, process a single thought.

She knows.

'But then, you always were a little peculiar, weren't you? Oh, well, never mind all that.' She folded her arms.

'Have you enjoyed your day so far? Did everything go exactly as you expected?'

Indigo realised he would have to speak, that he would have to say something.

'Would you mind leaving my room now, please, Peaches?' he said, almost in a whisper. 'I have things to do.'

'Of course, Indy. I just wanted to make sure you were OK. See you later!' She stared at him a moment longer, then turned to go. Her hand was on the doorknob when she stopped, turned back and said in a gentle voice: 'How's your leg, by the way?'

'What?'

Peaches pointed to his leg. Instinctively, Indigo straightened up.

'I noticed you had something of a limp recently.' The warmth left her voice. Her eyes, which seconds before had glowed warmly, became glassy and dead. 'As if something had bitten you. A spider, perhaps. A dancing spider.'

Indigo automatically backed up towards the window. 'I don't know what you're talking about,' he said. 'Really, Peaches, I ... have a ton of homework.'

Peaches, standing perfectly still, spoke in a voice that was so low, it came out no louder than a whisper. 'You think I don't know that you broke into my secret headquarters? I know. I know everything. When you hung outside my window, why, your little heart was beating so loudly I could scarcely hear myself think.'

As the fear churned inside him, threatening to drown everything else, Indigo McCloud searched for the little nugget of anger that had brought him to this point, the anger that had powered his fight against his sister's tyranny.

'I know what you did,' he said. 'You, Su and the twins. You tried to terrorise the Tripes the way you terrorised Lucy Jones. But Mandy never saw a single spider, did she? And Oswald got out before that stink sent him into a coma. All of your plans have come to nothing, Peaches. Game over. You lose.'

Peaches drew back in mock surprise. 'Listen to you!' she whispered. 'Here we were thinking you spent all your time mooning about up here with this old junk.' She wrinkled her nose at Indigo's tattered books and reclaimed furniture. 'But it turns out you were out saving the world. Such heroism!'

Indigo struggled to keep the anger alive. 'The Tripes –'

Peaches snorted. 'Oh, who cares about the Tripes? They'll get their just deserts eventually. You think your little heroics will make any difference?' She shook her head, smiling coldly. 'You've bought them a little time, that's all. But the truth is, little brother, that anyone who gets in my way pays the price. It's just the way it is. Ask Lucy.' Now she put on a look of mock concern. 'Oh, no, you can't ask Lucy, cos she's a gibbering wreck who can't leave her room.'

Indigo felt anger surge through him. 'What did she do? What did she do? She just refused to be bullied!' His voice rose as he spoke. 'And you crushed her!'

Peaches took a step closer, her eyes wide. Indigo fought the urge to move backwards. When she spoke, her voice was scarcely above a whisper. 'Bullied? What a silly little word. The truth is far simpler. She was given a job and she refused to do it.'

'Refused to do it? She –'

'Ah, but she came to you for help, didn't she, Indigo? Yes, she did, I know that. But you were too scared. Too *chicken*,' she hissed. 'You're doing all this because you feel guilty, and you feel guilty because you're weak.'

Indigo reached inside himself for the anger and clung to it.

'You're evil, Peaches, evil to the bone!' He realised he was shouting now, but he couldn't stop himself. 'What you did to Lucy was unspeakable! But I'm watching you now. You'll never terrorise anyone ever again!'

And then something very peculiar happened.

Peaches took a step back. Her chin wobbled, and her eyes became shiny with tears. 'Oh, Indy!' she cried. 'How could you say that?' Throwing back her head, she let out a long, forlorn wail.

For the second time that evening, Indigo went completely still.

'Daddy!' she cried. 'Daddy!'

The bedroom door swung open and there stood Tim McCloud, a tea-towel in one hand, a soup ladle in the other. His long hair hung about a mouth that dangled open.

'Oh, Daddy!' Peaches wept, launching herself into his arms so that he was forced to drop the ladle. 'It's much worse than we imagined!'

Tim stared at his son with the same unblinking shock and distractedly dabbed at his daughter's hair with the tea-towel.

'Oh, Daddy.' Peaches jabbed her finger in Indigo's direction. 'We have to do something to help him.' Though her head was pressed against her father's chest, Indigo saw her blue eyes flash like blades. 'For Mummy's sake,' she added.

At the mention of Indigo's mother, the corners of his father's eyes and mouth drooped, his shoulders wilted. Behind Tim, on the landing, Root, Berry and Su appeared, their faces talcum-powder pale, their eyes wet. A faint whiff of chopped onions permeated the air.

And now Indigo understood. It was a trap. It was all a trap. And he had fallen headlong into it.

'Dad, I … She …'

He didn't know how to continue. He was caught; he was exposed. He stared at his father, and his father stared back. Peaches was Tim's pride and joy, his golden princess, his everything. To expose her, to show her for what she really was – it could destroy him. But if she wasn't stopped … Indigo ceased thinking. Instinct took over.

'She's … Dad, she's not how she appears, please believe me … Look.'

He came out onto the landing, pushed past them all and went into the girls' room. Dropping to the floor, he groped under Root's bed for the lever.

The lever wasn't there.

Tim came slowly into the room. 'You said she was … she was evil, Indigo,' he said slowly. 'I heard you. *Evil*. What did you mean?'

Indigo peered under the bed. The lever was gone. 'There's this underground lair, where Peaches and the girls …' Even as he spoke, he knew that he had lost. She had covered her tracks completely. 'There's a …' He wanted to say a hit list, but knew that by saying those words, he would only dig himself deeper. How had they done it? He seized the cluttered pink dressing table and pulled it out of the way.

'Hey!' said Root. 'Stop messing with our stuff!'

Behind the dressing table there was nothing but bare floorboards. They were smooth and clean and innocent.

'It was right here,' said Indigo, staring.

'An underground lair?' his father repeated. 'Did I hear you right? An underground lair?'

'Dad,' said Indigo, 'I know it's …'

Tim stared at his son as if he'd never seen him before. 'What's come over you, Indigo?'

'An underground lair, Dad!' Peaches wailed. 'An underground lair! It's even worse than I thought!' She glanced back at the girls. 'And so upsetting for the little ones!'

On cue, the twins began to whimper theatrically.

'It's not your fault, Dad,' Root said with a sniff. 'Indigo was always a nasty little liar.'

'Hey!' said Berry. '*I* was going to say that.'

'Everybody just … just stop,' said their father. 'I need to talk to you alone, Indigo. Downstairs, now.'

'Dad, I –'

'Please, Indigo. Downstairs.'

The second Tim's back was turned, each of the girls turned hideous, triumphant grins on Indigo. Root shook with suppressed laughter. Berry poked him hard in the back. Su drew her nunchucks from behind her back and twirled them above her head. Behind them all, Peaches raised a hand and slowly waved. *Bye bye*, she mouthed.

Downstairs in the kitchen, his father indicated to Indigo that he should sit.

'Dad, listen, I know this sounds a bit crazy, but –'

His father, sitting down at the rickety table opposite him, seized on these words. 'Exactly, Indigo, exactly! I'm glad you put it like that. A bit crazy. Exactly. I mean, when Peaches told me about what you had been saying, I thought, there's no way –'

'Wait a second,' said Indigo, 'are you telling me that she's talked to you about this before now?'

Tim pulled his glasses from his face, leaving it looking naked and exposed. 'She came to me first a week ago. She told me you had been accusing her of all kinds of things.'

'A week ago?'

'Naturally, I thought she was ... well, I never disbelieved her, of course, but the things she was telling me! That you were accusing her of *harming* other children? Well, I mean, she would never.'

And now a sudden realisation came crashing into Indigo's head. *There's a plan.*

Peaches, he realised, had set a plan in motion, a plan just as diabolical, just as complex as those she had made for Lucy and the Tripes. Except this time, *he* was at the centre of it.

Tim replaced his spectacles on his nose and stood up. He coughed. 'You know, son,' he said, 'there's this great place you can go, if you ... you know, have a bit of a problem with the truth.'

'What?' Indigo, consumed by the realisation of just how badly he had been duped, hadn't really heard his father.

'It's great,' Tim went on. 'It was Peaches who found out about it, actually. She's just so worried about you. It's a place,' he coughed again, 'for boys like you who need a bit of discipline, a bit of structure. A place where they help you to stop all this horrible lying.'

Indigo stood up. 'Dad, listen. You've got to listen to me.'

Tim went to the counter and picked up the leaflet that lay there. Glancing down at it, he began falteringly: 'It … it sounds like the perfect place to, you know, get over this nasty little phase.'

It was at this moment that Indigo noticed the packed bag that stood by the door, with his jacket draped over it.

'Dad.'

Tim held up the leaflet. There was a picture of a long, military-type building behind a tall fence topped with razor wire.

Just then, there was a knock at the door.

'Ah,' said his father, 'that'll be them.'

15

The Sudden Arrival
of Captain Grotty

'That'll be who?'

'It's only for a short while, Indy,' said his father, moving backwards towards the front door. 'Just until you – you know – get over it.'

He turned and opened the door. There on the doorstep stood two men. Both were wearing military clothes. One was short and thin, with greasy slicked-back hair. He snapped to attention.

'Mr McCloud, I presume?'

'Ah … yes.'

'My name is … eh …' The man's mind seemed to go suddenly blank. He stared into the house. 'Captain Grotty,' he said, smiling uncertainly. 'And this is …' Scanning the kitchen, the man took in all of Su's trophies. 'Eh … Private Winner.'

He indicated the second man, who was tall and very strongly built. The backs of Private Winner's hands were covered in tattoos, and his large shaved head emerged from the collar of his army jacket like that of a bull. Stooping,

Winner peered past Indigo's father into the interior of the house.

Indigo didn't respond for a moment. He was staring at the van, which stood by the kerb just outside the house. It was old, rusty and covered in flakes of peeling black and amber paint. The aerial was gone. In its place, someone had fixed a wire coat-hanger pulled into a diamond shape. The worst thing, however, the thing that made Indigo feel as though all his bones had been replaced by slush, was the writing. In dauby red paint, somebody – somebody who was not particularly good at writing – had scrawled the following words across the side of the van: 'Blunt Home for Nasty Little Liars'. The paint was still wet. Long trails of red dripped from the last two words, making them look blood-like.

'And you must be Indigo,' said Captain Grotty, pushing in through the front door and darting over to Indigo. 'Terrible thing, Mr McCloud, when a young man goes bad, eh? So painful when he starts lying through his teeth about his wonderful older sister.'

Though Grotty was slight – not much bigger, in fact, than Indigo himself – he was so full of nervous energy that he looked as though he might explode at any minute. Indigo could not drag his eyes from the silver tooth that glinted at the front of the man's mouth. And the man himself seemed unable to drag his gaze from Indigo.

'But don't you worry, Mr McCloud. By the time we're finished with him, he'll never tell a lie again, will he, Private Winner?'

'Ooh! Look!' The huge bull-headed man lumbered into the kitchen and went straight to the cooker. He began straightening up Su's trophies. 'Bad luck having trophies facing the wrong way! Gotta all face out!'

'Very superstitious, Private Winner,' said Captain Grotty, still staring at Indigo. 'Never goes anywhere without his lucky onion. Isn't that right, Private Winner?'

'Oh, yeah!' said Private Winner, producing a small withered union from the pocket of his coat. 'Never go anywhere without me onion!' He returned it quickly to his pocket, picked up another of Su's trophies and began peering at the inscription at its base. His lips moved as he read. 'Resting,' he said. 'You can get trophies for resting now?'

Tim came over and took the trophy from the man's hands. 'Wrestling,' he said, looking uncertainly at the huge man. 'It's for wrestling.'

'Ah!' said the man, nodding vigorously. 'Wrestling's a lot tougher than resting! Why, I was sitting on this chap's head one time and –'

'Thank you, Private Winner,' said Captain Grotty, hastily talking over his colleague. 'While I do love to hear your stamp-collecting stories, I think it's time we were all on our way.'

'Dad,' said Indigo, 'look at these people. They're not who they say they are.'

Anger flickered across the features of the small greasy-haired man. 'Oh, we're *exactly* who we say we are, son,' he said, laying a hand on Indigo's shoulder and leaning in to his face. The man's breath smelled strongly of peppermint. 'We're going to make sure you never tell another lie as long as you live.'

Tim McCloud glanced doubtfully at the leaflet he still held in his hand, then looked up at the two men. 'Can you tell me something about what you do in this place?'

Indigo seized on his father's uncertainty. 'Yeah, do, tell us something about that, Captain Grotty.'

But now there was a rush of movement from the top of the stairs and down came Peaches, followed closely by her sisters. 'Oh, thank goodness you're here!' she cried. 'It's a wonderful place, Daddy! And Indigo must go to the very best!'

'Absolutely!' said the thin man brightly, squeezing Indigo's shoulder and staring at him with eyes that glinted with a strange and unsettling light, as if the brain behind them was full of strange and unsettling thoughts. 'By the time we're done with him, he'll only have good things to say about his wonderful older sister.'

'Oh, Indigo!' Peaches threw her arms around her brother. 'You know I love you, don't you? You'll be back with us really soon, I know you will!'

As she hugged him, Peaches whispered into Indigo's ear, 'You should know that very soon your precious Tripes will be gone for ever. In one hour's time, there won't be a single one from here to Cragmire. No-one will ever see them again.'

Before Indigo could say anything, Peaches leaped back from him, her face contorted in imaginary pain. 'Oh,

Indigo, how could you say such a thing!' Covering her face with her hands, she ran to her father, who automatically hugged his daughter. 'Daddy, he said the most horrible thing! I can't repeat it!'

'Dad!' said Indigo. 'Don't listen to her! It's not true!'

His father stared at him in shock. 'Indigo! What ... what's come over you?'

'Oh, poor Indy!' Peaches wailed. 'The sooner he gets there, Daddy, the sooner he'll be cured.'

Biting back tears, Tim nodded slowly. 'I think you should go, Indigo.'

'Yes, come along now, son,' said Captain Grotty, guiding Indigo firmly towards the front door.

'Dad,' said Indigo, 'this is crazy.'

Before his father could reply, Peaches increased the pitch of her sobbing. 'Oh, Dad, why does he hate me? Why did he say those horrible things?'

'Just please go, Indigo.' His father's voice was choked with emotion. 'We'll ... see you ... soon.'

Thinking quickly, Indigo allowed his shoulders to sag. At the door, he pulled on his jacket as Private Winner scooped up his bag. He did not resist when Captain Grotty led him out into the street and around to the back of the van. As his family streamed out onto the street after him, he did everything he could in those few short steps to give the impression that he had been defeated, that he accepted his fate; that he would not run.

Then he ran.

'Indigo!' his father called after him. 'Please, Indy, stop! INDY!'

But Indigo McCloud knew that he couldn't stop. There was little doubt that Peaches had something horrible in store for him. He had to protect himself. He had to run.

At the end of the terrace, he turned left, then left again. Glancing backwards, he could see the huge bull-headed man, perhaps twenty metres back, but closing on him. The man was fit and fast, despite his size.

Indigo's first instinct was to get up on to the roofs as quickly as possible. As he ran, he scanned the street for a way up. None would present itself.

He turned sharply down a narrow alley that wound between the backs of houses, half-hoping that the man would miss the turn and overshoot. He did not. The way was strewn with long grass, weeds and clutter, old bikes and abandoned washing machines, all grey and streaked from the smoky drizzle. Indigo leaped these with ease. His pursuer, however, struggled to maintain his pace as he navigated each successive obstacle. When Indigo emerged out onto Mange Close, he still could see no way upwards. Instead, he made a snap decision. Both sides of the close were lined with parked cars. Indigo darted across the street to an orange Ford, got down on the sodden tarmac and rolled. Once he made it under the car, he stopped dead and held his breath.

He could feel the pounding feet through the tarmac as the man emerged onto Mange Close and stopped, scanning the way up and down. Indigo knew what the bull-headed man was thinking. Had the boy made it to the end of the close and away, or was he hiding here? From where he lay, Indigo could not see the man's bull-like head, but he could see the huge body with its great dangling arms and the backs of his hands with their collection of dark tattoos.

The man came rushing towards the car beneath which Indigo lay. Indigo fought the urge to make a break for it. There was no way he would be able to roll, get to his feet and run before he would be grabbed.

The feet stopped barely a centimetre from him. The toes of the man's highly polished black shoes – which were truly enormous – protruded under the car, almost touching Indigo's arm. He wore odd socks, one red and one green, and the lace of one of his huge shoes was untied. Indigo, still as a corpse, tried to make his heart beat more quietly as the man stood there, panting heavily.

'Hmmm,' he said to himself. 'Where did you go, eh?'

The huge feet shifted, bringing him and Indigo even closer.

'I think I'll toss a coin,' he said.

Indigo heard muffled tinkling sounds as the man went rummaging in his pockets. 'Heads, you hid, tails, you ran.'

Indigo flinched. If the toss went wrong, the man would begin checking the undersides of cars, starting with the one at which he stood. At any moment, that bull-like head would appear between the wheels and Indigo would be caught. Clenching his whole body, Indigo very silently and very slowly rolled out to the street side of the car, crept to the nearest wheel and, making himself as small as possible, he crouched there. He heard the *dink … whirr … tock* of a coin being tossed.

'Ha!' said the man. 'Ready or not, here I come!'

There was another scuffing sound as the man dropped onto his belly and scanned the undersides of the cars, staring into the space where Indigo had been mere seconds before. Indigo could smell the man's sweat; he could practically feel his eyes.

Then he heard a grunt of annoyance. The man stood up and took off down Mange Close at speed. As he ran, Indigo remained where he was, watching the man's huge retreating back. *Don't look back*, Indigo thought, *don't look back*.

He did not look back.

As soon as the man disappeared around the corner, Indigo stood up. The week's rain had left the street greasy and damp. Indigo's runners were wet from the long grass of the alleyway. The temperature had dropped. He shivered.

Peaches had outwitted him completely. She had known exactly what he was doing all along. How? His mind teemed with questions. Who were those men? Where had they planned to take him? How was he going to convince his father that he wasn't lying? *I can't go home*, he thought despondently. For a moment, self-pity swamped Indigo McCloud. For a moment, he stood in the damp, run-down street and felt utterly empty.

I can't go home, he thought again, and then he added a single word. *Yet*.

He would go home, but only when he had done what he set out to do. He would stop Peaches. Despite the fear and the sorrow, Indigo had the overwhelming sense that, for the first time in his life, he was doing the right thing. Standing up to Peaches was terrifying, but there was no going back now. He had survived in the past by hiding from her, but now he had stepped out into the open. The only way forward was through Peaches. He had to stop her. Had to.

You should know that very soon your precious Tripes will be gone for ever. In one hour's time, there won't be a single one from here to Cragmire. No-one will ever see them again.

What had she planned? *From here to Cragmire.* That meant the cousins, the ones who had helped Mandy sell so many calendars. How many had Polly said there were? Twenty-seven. *No-one will ever see them again.* What was she going to do with them?

Indigo knew that the two horrible men would not give up the chase; if they did, they would have Peaches to answer to. They would continue to prowl the streets until they found him. He had to get to Polly's. There was so much to figure out, so much to try to process. There was no way, however, that he could go back the way he had come. The only alternative was to find a way onto the roofs and make his way back to Adenoid Terrace that way.

Mange Street lay around the corner from Mange Close. It was a long row of identical red-brick houses, just like Adenoid Terrace. But towards the end, it adjoined a patch of waste ground on which Blunt Municipal Baths had once stood. The baths had been closed down and demolished some years earlier, after they had become infested with flesh-eating shrimp. Nothing had since been done with the site, apart from the erection of a high wall all around the perimeter. Indigo knew that if he could get there without being caught, he could then climb to the roofs and make his way unseen to Polly's house. There, he and Polly could figure out what to do next.

Unfortunately, going down Mange Street was the worst decision Indigo had made all day. It was at this moment that Chief Inspector Milkweed re-entered proceedings.

Since the discovery of the scrap of Indigo's jacket at the breadcrumb factory, Milkweed had personally led Blunt's police dog-handling team about the town, trying to pick up the scent of the Breadcrumb Bandit. So it was that, as Indigo neared the wall which he hoped would lead him to the roofs, who should come around the corner but Chief Inspector Milkweed, two dog handlers and two large German shepherds.

The dogs had already picked up Indigo's scent before they rounded the corner and were straining against their leashes and barking loudly when they turned in to Mange Street and saw Indigo McCloud – still quite a distance away – climbing onto the wall. The first time Milkweed had seen Indigo had been in the smoky twilight of the breadcrumb factory, and he had been too far away to get a proper look at his face. The dogs' reaction, however, left the policeman in no doubt as to who it was.

'THERE HE IS!' boomed Milkweed. 'THE BREAD-CRUMB BANDIT! GET HIM! GET HIM! GET HIM!'

Indigo shot along the top of the wall and in two leaps was on the roof of the nearest house. He scrambled up to the top and scampered across the peak at speed, while down below him, the dogs barked and the policemen shouted instructions to each other. Halfway down the street, he changed direction, slid down the roof, flipped onto the top of a dividing wall and padded speedily across to the back of an adjoining street, where, once again, he hauled himself up onto the roof. The policemen tried to follow him from the ground, but Indigo, keeping low and moving quickly, was able to outpace them. Within minutes, they were running about Mange Street and its adjoining alleyways blindly, while Indigo quietly made his way back towards Adenoid Terrace and Polly's house.

Keeping to the roofs that faced away from the street, Indigo flitted across the slates, hardly making a sound, as the barking of the dogs grew ever more distant. He arrived onto Brain Street and checked the street on both sides. There was no sign of either the two horrible men or the police.

But just as he was about to turn the corner onto the terrace, something moved behind him. He tried to dodge out of the way, but he was too late. Thin arms clamped him from behind, so that Indigo could not move.

'Your sister told me you might try something like this.' The voice brought with it the whiff of peppermint. Captain Grotty. Indigo turned his head and saw the harness connecting the man to the chimney behind which he had hidden. The arms tightened, driving all of the air out of Indigo's lungs.

'You know what I do with this silver tooth?' the thin man whispered into Indigo's ear. 'I bite things. I bite things *off*. When we get where we're going, you're going to lose … hmmm … let's say … two, yes, *two* of your fingers. That's, of course, assuming you survive the fall.'

And with that, the man heaved Indigo off the roof.

16

The Witch Pig of Bo

Just as these dreadful things were happening to Indigo, a short distance away, in Number 43, the assembled Tripe cousins were thronging the kitchen, enjoying a late lunch.

Oswald had, of course, returned home earlier that day. The mystery buffs Hortense and Aurelia ran into him on Eek Street not long after he had left the factory and were more than happy to claim credit for finding him. As soon as he arrived into Number 43, his huge extended family surged around him, then surged suddenly back when they caught a whiff of the dreadful odours that still hung about him.

Mandy quickly drew up a rota, and soon there were three teams of Tripes taking it in turns to scrub Oswald clean. Mr Tripe and Little Molly took the clothes that he had been wearing and, with novelty clothes-pegs on their noses, they lit a small fire in the back yard and burned them all.

Afterwards, the extended Tripe clan crowded into the kitchen for a celebratory lunch. As they tucked into the remaining German sausage and home-made bread, Mr Tripe collected the post from the stand in the hall. It had been forgotten in the chaos and bustle of the morning's events, but now Mr Tripe returned to the kitchen, shuffling the assortment of envelopes through his hands and shaking his head.

'Dear, oh dear, three final demands today. Electricity, gas and phone. Dear, oh dear.' His face brightened. 'Ooh, look, darling, the new brochure for Grimwald's Novelty Clocks! Let's pick one out right away!'

Mrs Tripe, her mouth full of brown bread and marmalade, clapped her hands delightedly.

Oswald and Mandy looked at each other.

'Dad,' said Mandy, 'I really think you should look at those bills first. Perhaps if –'

'Hang on,' said her father. 'There's one for you here, Mandy. Looks important!'

He handed the silver envelope to his daughter, who stared at it wordlessly. One of her cousins passed her a clean knife. She carefully cut open the top of the envelope and pulled out a letter. Opening it up, she read the first few words and her eyes widened in delight.

'I've won it!' she cried, jumping up. 'I've won the bike!'

The kitchen exploded into applause and whoops of delight as the Tripes crowded about Mandy, the ones towards the edges craning their necks to catch a glimpse of the letter.

'Oh, my dear, that's wonderful!' Mrs Tripe exclaimed, hugging her daughter.

'Fantastic!' said Mr Tripe. 'Well done, Mandy.'

Mandy scanned the rest of the letter. 'It says that they're going to present it to me today! And there's more … There's to be a "novelty surprise trip down the River Blunt".

Wow! A novelty surprise trip! Imagine! It says, "for you and everyone who supported you in your calendar sales".'

Mandy looked around at her cousins. 'Why, that's all of you. Gosh! I wonder if there'll be enough room.'

She looked again at the letter. 'No, wait! It says there's space for twenty-nine people! Why, that's exactly the right number! Isn't that fantastic? You hear that, everyone? We're all going on a novelty surprise trip on the Blunt!'

Another resounding cheer greeted these words. The cousins celebrated by punching the air and doing high fives. In the midst of the happy hubbub, someone launched into the Tripe family song, 'Tripes! Tripes! Tripes!', and soon everyone joined in. By the time the nineteenth and final verse was over, the crowd was in very high spirits and the kitchen rang with laughter and happy talk.

'That's just wonderful, Mandy!' Her father had to shout to make himself heard. 'What kind of novelty surprise trip is it exactly?'

* * *

Indigo McCloud had leaped from roofs many times before and landed without injury. It was one thing, however, to execute a safe landing from a well-timed leap. It was quite another to do so after you are flung bodily from the roof of a two-storey building by a psychopathic thug hired by your sister to kidnap you.

Indigo went pitching backwards, his arms flailing, the world a whirling blur all around him. He tried to turn over, tried to regain control. He knew that unless something

127

miraculous happened, serious injury was almost certain. If he struck his head, he would probably die. He had to turn, he had to get control. He caught sight of the grey pavement rushing towards him, then all of a sudden something struck his side, then his leg. He cried out in pain and his head was flung backwards. The air left his lungs. Huge arms wrapped about him.

'Gotcha!' said a voice. 'I caught him, Ern!'

'Get him in the van!' came the reply from the roof.

Indigo kicked his legs and tried to right himself but the arms crushed him. He heard a door creak open and he was flung into the back of the van as though he weighed no more than a packet of crisps. He cried out as his side struck the floor, but still tried to turn, to get back out before the door shut. Now, however, the large blank face of the bull-headed man rose above him. There would be no escape.

'You're for it, son, when we get to … well, when we get where we're goin'.' He held up his huge tattoo-covered hand and wriggled his fingers. 'By the time Ern's finished with you, you won't be playing the piano no more.'

And with that, he slammed the door shut.

Indigo kicked at it. The thud echoed briefly, but the door did not budge. Still sprawled on the floor, he aimed another kick at the side. There was another thud but not the slightest hint of give. Panting, trying to coax the air back into his lungs, he righted himself, wincing at the pain that ran up his side to his shoulder.

There was a small grille at the front of the van which gave into the driver's cab. This was the only opening and the source of the dim light which penetrated Indigo's prison.

'Help!' Indigo called out, his voice weak. 'HELP!' He kicked again and again against the side of the van.

The passenger door of the cab opened, then the driver's door, and both Private Winner and Captain Grotty got in. The smaller man didn't turn around, but called back as he put the key in the ignition. 'Make as much noise as you like, kid – this thing is soundproofed. No-one can hear you scream.'

He gunned the engine and the van sped off, throwing Indigo painfully against the back doors. They drove rapidly through the streets of the town, sending him pitching this way and that. He stopped kicking, stopped shouting, stopped struggling. There was no point. He had to think of something else – but all that he could think was that he had lost.

He had lost, Peaches had won, and there was nothing now to stop her from doing whatever she wanted to. He thought again of what she had said about the Tripes. *No-one will ever see them again.* Within the next hour, twenty-nine children would somehow disappear, Peaches would control Adenoid Terrace like never before and Indigo would have two of his fingers bitten off.

He closed his eyes, opened them again, then got to his feet, edged forward and managed to brace himself against the front of the van. He peered through the grille.

Captain Grotty was driving. Private Winner sat with a newspaper held close to his face. He was, Indigo saw, reading out the other one's horoscope, or trying to.

'"Your poise and grace have not gone unnoticed by a significant someone." Ooooh! Hear that, Ern? Your poise and grace, they haven't gone unnoticed. Hang on, there's more. "The new moon on Tuesday could give you the perfect opportunity to snuggle up with that special someone." Now, that's nice, right, Ern?'

'Drop it, Vern,' said Captain Grotty coldly. 'No-one but a fool like you believes that twaddle. There's nothing dumber than – No! Not those stupid cards again!'

Private Winner had put the paper away and had taken out a deck of large cards, decorated with all kinds of curious images and symbols. 'These cards is very powerful, Ern, very powerful. They never let me down. Always full of hints about what the future will bring.'

'No, they aren't, you moron. They're just a load of stupid, meaningless pictures.'

But Winner had already lost interest in the conversation and was carefully laying the cards out along the dashboard of the van. 'Oh, look, Ern, the Weeping Swamp Rat. He don't mean much on his own. I'll try another. Ah! Now that's the Blue Sofa with the Red Cushions. Nice. Hmm, still not sure what it all means, though. Hang on, the third one will reveal everything.'

The next card, Indigo saw through the grille, depicted a large black pig wearing a tall pointed hat. Turning it over appeared to have a curious effect on Private Winner. He stared at the card in fright.

'The Witch Pig of Bo,' he breathed eventually. 'It's the Witch Pig of Bo, Ern.'

'So what?'

'So what? So what? The Witch Pig is the worst card ever! It means doom, Ern, DOOM!'

In the back of the van, the darkness was suddenly illuminated by an invisible lightbulb which came on directly over Indigo McCloud's head. He had had an idea.

17

The Terrible Teeth
of Captain Grotty

'He's right!' Indigo shouted. 'There's no worse card than the Witch Pig of Bo.'

'You stay out of it!' Captain Grotty snarled. 'Enjoy your fingers while you can.'

'You know the cards?' Private Winner turned back and squinted at the prisoner.

'Sure!' said Indigo. 'Nothing worse than the Witch Pig – unless of course …'

'Don't listen to him, Vern,' said Captain Grotty.

Private Winner stared at the Witch Pig silently for a moment, then he turned back to Indigo. 'Unless of course what?'

'I said don't listen to him.' Grotty elbowed Winner in the ribs.

'Oh, it doesn't matter,' said Indigo. 'I'm probably wrong.'

Private Winner shifted in his seat. 'Unless what?' he said, more loudly.

'Well, if I were you, I'd turn over another card.'

'You think?' said Winner, scratching his temple. Indigo noted that he had the names of various animals tattooed along his fingers: 'Soaring Eagle' was one. 'Savage Lion' was another, except 'Lion' had been misspelled as 'Lino'.

'Yes, definitely,' said Indigo, pressing up against the grille and trying to sound like he knew what he was talking about.

'He doesn't know anything about your stupid cards, you idiot!' said Grotty. 'Next thing, he's going to tell you that the stupid cards want you to let him go, and give him a few quid while you're at it.'

Private Winner turned over another card, revealing a three-legged spider carrying some sort of brush.

'There!' said Indigo. 'What did I tell you?'

From where Indigo crouched, peering into the cab, he could not see Winner's face, but he could tell that the man was staring at the card with a puzzled expression.

'The Three-Legged Spider with the Toilet Brush?' said Winner. 'I thought that meant you should avoid wearing yellow wellies until after the new moon.'

'Well, sure!' said Indigo. 'Ordinarily, of course, that's exactly what it means, but coming straight after the Witch Pig of Bo, well, it's a rejection card, isn't it? It defeats the Witch Pig. Well ... it defeats the Witch Pig most of the time anyway.'

'He's having you on, you dingbat!' said Captain Grotty, becoming more agitated.

Winner turned back to Indigo, scowling. 'How'd you know all this?'

'You never studied confirmation and rejection cards?' said Indigo. 'My dad taught me all about them; he's an expert.'

Indigo watched Private Winner process this information. Scowling deeply, he replayed the words that Indigo had said, moving his lips slowly as he did so.

'That crusty-looking chap with the long hair? An expert?'

'Don't tell me you never heard of Tim McCloud!' said Indigo incredulously. 'He's only the foremost authority on the cards in the country. Haven't you read his books?'

Winner shook his head.

'He's lying to you!' Captain Grotty shouted. 'It's all lies!'

'Wait a sec,' said Private Winner, 'you said the Three-Legged Spider with the Toilet Brush beats the Witch Pig of Bo *most of the time*, right?'

'Yup,' said Indigo, 'nothing to worry about so long as you're not wearing odd socks.'

Private Winner froze, his eyes widened and he looked from Indigo to Captain Grotty. 'I am wearing odd socks, I am!'

'What?' said Indigo. 'That's terrible!' He turned to Grotty. 'Stop the van! We've got to get away from him as soon as possible.'

Captain Grotty laughed. 'You always wear odd socks, you clot! He saw 'em earlier.'

Winner had started to panic. 'Did he?' he asked uncertainly.

'The cards have cursed him!' Indigo shouted. 'If you draw the Witch Pig of Bo followed by the Three-Legged Spider with the Toilet Brush while wearing odd socks, it means you've done something terrible! It means terrible retribution will follow!'

'SHUDDUP!' yelled Captain Grotty. The van swerved as he ineffectually elbowed the grille.

Indigo did not shut up. 'It is called …' he paused for effect '… the Unlacing.'

'What?' said Private Winner.

'It's a horrible death,' said Indigo, almost whispering now. 'The Pig and the Spider pull you apart from the inside.'

'No!' said Private Winner, now clearly terrified.

'Prove it!' Captain Grotty shouted. 'Prove it, you nasty, snot-nosed little brat!'

'The Unlacing starts at the feet,' said Indigo quietly. 'Check your laces – that's how it always starts.'

Indigo saw Private Winner gulp, then slowly bend over to inspect his feet. It had been perhaps half an hour since he had seen the enormous man's odd socks and untied lace from his hiding place underneath the car. It was quite possible – quite likely even – that the man had tied the lace since then. But if he hadn't …

'It's untied! I'm doomed!' Winner wailed. 'DOOMED!'

'I'll doom you, you pillock!' Captain Grotty shouted. 'He wants you to let him go, doesn't he? He'll say anything.'

'It's the Unlacing, Ern! The Unlacing!'

'You can probably feel the tingle in your feet by now,' Indigo put in.

'I CAN! OOOH, I CAN, I CAN.' The big man lifted his leg and, pulling off his shoe, he began massaging a red-socked foot. 'OOOOH, ERN! IT'S TINGLING!'

By now, the van had left Blunt behind and was speeding

through the countryside along the Cragmire road. A thick line of trees ran along one side, while rolling farmland and empty fields of grass lay on the opposite side.

'RIGHT!' said Captain Grotty. He suddenly braked hard, sending everyone pitching forward, then swerved into the side of the road and hauled up the handbrake. He turned to Private Winner. 'There is no such thing as the Witch Pig of bleeding Bo, and there is no such thing as the stupid spider with the bleeding whatever. This kid knows he's done for, so he's trying to convince you that he knows stuff about your stupid cards so you'll let him go. And you fell for it, you great big brainless wonder.'

Captain Grotty turned to Indigo, his eyes blazing with the same strange and unsettling light. 'Your sister asked us to keep you for a bit,' he said quietly. 'She did not say that you had to come back in one piece.' He bared his silver tooth. 'It's finger-biting time.'

'I've only seen the Unlacing once before,' Indigo went on. 'It took hours. The guy screamed and screamed.'

'SHUDDUP!' Grotty struck the grille. He turned to Private Winner, who had grown very pale and was still holding his foot. 'You hold him while I do it,' he said, opening the door of the van. Then, more to himself than anyone else, he added, 'This'll shut him up.'

'You must have done something truly terrible to be cursed with the Unlacing,' said Indigo. 'There's almost no way out of it.'

'Almost?' said Private Winner, in a curiously high-pitched voice.

'You'd have to do somebody a good turn, but it would have to be a really, really good turn. You'd almost have to save someone's life. You can probably feel it in the other foot now,' said Indigo.

'Oooh, I CAN!' said Winner, grabbing his other foot as Captain Grotty wrenched open the back doors of the van.

The small man stood there, his eyes glinting, and flexed his fingers. Every muscle in his body seemed primed to do something horrible. He smiled and the smell of peppermint filled Indigo's narrow prison.

'Times like this,' he said, 'I really do enjoy my work.'

His side still smarting from the fall, Indigo left the grille and backed himself into a corner.

'Get round here, you!' Captain Grotty called to Private Winner. Indigo heard the big man shuffle back into his shoes, then open the passenger door, climb out and slam it again. Captain Grotty, meanwhile, had climbed into the back of the van and was grinning broadly.

'Might as well get it over with, kid,' he said in a horrible sing-song voice. 'There's nothing you can do about it.'

Indigo kicked at the man's hands as he approached, but Grotty, quick as a whip, grabbed Indigo's ankle and dragged him rapidly to the back door. He tried to kick at the man's face to get himself loose, but Captain Grotty, who never stopped grinning, was too strong.

'I won't lie to you, kid – this is gonna hurt.' He lunged for Indigo's hand, once, twice, three times. On the fourth attempt he got it. 'Ha ha!' he cried and began drawing Indigo's hand towards his mouth.

Indigo lashed out with his foot and his free hand. Though he succeeded in landing a heavy blow on Captain Grotty's nose, the man did not let go.

He called over his shoulder, 'Get over here, you big –'

Captain Grotty did not finish the sentence because at that moment two huge hands seized him by the throat and swept him from the van.

'I'm sorry, Ern, I can't let you do that,' said Private Winner.

'GET OFF, YOU STUPID …' Captain Grotty tried to wriggle free from Private Winner's clutches but the big man had gripped him in a bear hug from which he could not escape. 'WHAT DO YOU THINK YOU'RE DOING?' Captain Grotty roared, his eyes bulging, his face purple with rage.

'Get out of here, kid, fast as you can,' said Private Winner.

Indigo did not need to be asked twice. He scrambled from the van as Captain Grotty gnashed his teeth and roared with rage.

'I'll MURDER YOU! I'LL BITE OFF YOUR NOSE!'

'I'll bet that tingling is easing now?' said Indigo

Private Winner looked down at Indigo over the struggling Captain Grotty. His eyes brightened and he nodded vigorously. 'It is, it is!'

Indigo nodded sagely. 'The Unlacing has been halted because of your good works.'

'You hear that, Ern?' said Private Winner excitedly. 'I'm saved!'

'I'M GONNA KILL YOU TOO. YOU –'

Caught up in their struggle against each other, neither

Captain Grotty nor Private Winner noticed that Indigo did not set out towards Blunt. Instead, he disappeared around the front of the van, then very cautiously and very quietly he opened the driver's door and climbed inside, pulled it slowly closed and locked it. He reached across and carefully locked the passenger door.

Peaches had said that the Tripes would be gone for ever within the hour. And that was almost an hour ago. The only hope of getting back to town in time was by driving.

Indigo had never driven anything before.

He grabbed the keys, which dangled from the ignition, and turned them briskly. The engine came alive.

Unseen behind the van, the struggle between Captain Grotty and Private Winner froze momentarily as both men tried to process the fact someone had just turned on the engine of their van.

Grotty was the first to come to a conclusion. 'He's stealing our van!'

'Eh?' said Winner.

'Our van, our van, he's stealing our van! I told you he was having you on!'

'Stealing our van?' said Private Winner, suddenly loosening his grip. 'I'll kill him.'

Indigo looked at the three pedals under his feet and tried to remember which one was which. He knew that you had to press one of them to move the gear stick, and that you had to move the gear stick to get the van going, but how to sequence all of this? He tried a couple of combinations, grabbed the gear stick and shoved it into what he hoped was first gear. As he did, there was a terrible grinding noise, the van lurched forward and the engine died.

Captain Grotty appeared suddenly at Indigo's window. 'By the time I finish with you,' he roared, 'you won't have a finger left to pick your horrible little nose, or a nose left to get picked!'

Private Winner's enormous head now filled the other window. He seized the handle of the door and began trying to pull it off its hinges.

Indigo turned the keys again and the engine came back to life. He tried another pedal, shoved the van into first gear, then released the pedal again. Too quickly. The van lurched forward, bucking and heaving. This time, however, the engine did not die. The two men continued to cling to the doors as Indigo spun the steering wheel, sending the van arcing out onto the road. An oncoming car blared its horn and swerved to avoid it.

'Ayyyyyeeee!' Captain Grotty wailed.

Private Winner began head-butting the passenger-door window as Indigo pressed the accelerator all the way to the floor. The engine roared, he inexpertly shifted gear and once again the van heaved and bucked. Private Winner clung doggedly to the handle, while Captain Grotty was thrown sideways into the road. Glancing to the left, Indigo saw Private Winner's huge face set in stony determination. As the bucking eased, the enormous man wrenched at the handle. Indigo felt the whole van lurch sideways.

Captain Grotty, meanwhile, had scrambled to his feet and was back at Indigo's window, howling obscenities.

Indigo pressed down on the clutch, shifted the van into first gear, then, having learned his lesson, he *slowly* eased up the clutch. This time, the van did not buck, but began accelerating rapidly. The engine roared and, concentrating hard, Indigo found second gear. Now, with an anguished cry, Captain Grotty disappeared from the window. Private Winner was struggling to keep pace. His face was reddening as he clung to the handle. The passenger door creaked and seemed to bow outwards, but now Indigo found third gear. Private Winner, without so much as a whisper, went flying backwards. Looking in the rear-view mirror, Indigo watched him pick himself up and stand in the middle of the road, panting and staring silently after the van.

18

The Uncertain Victory
of Mandy Tripe

The woman in charge of the novelty surprise trip down the Blunt wore a plum-coloured trouser suit, a plum-coloured shirt and a plum-coloured tie, with a neatly folded plum-coloured handkerchief poking up from her breast pocket. A long plum-coloured cape hung about her shoulders and her long hair, which was silvery grey, was piled high on her head and held in place with many hair accessories. Mandy found it difficult to tell what age she was. From one angle she appeared quite young; from another, her face seemed weathered and old. The woman stood at the bottom of the hatch as each Tripe came down the steps, watching them through large saffron-coloured eyes.

'Come along now, darlings!' she called. 'And do be careful! What should I do if one of you suffered a fall?'

The woman, who had introduced herself as Ms Follicle, reached out and patted each arriving curly head warmly and smiled a very strange smile. Mandy couldn't quite put her finger on why the smile seemed so peculiar, nor could she decide whether it was a good peculiar or a bad peculiar. This uncertainty unsettled her, so she did her best to shrug it off.

A submarine on the River Blunt! she thought. *What fun!*

It was fortunate that everyone was available to take part in the trip at such short notice. Except it was far more cramped than she had imagined. And all of them had been herded into the back of the vessel, where there was nothing really to see except the grey steel interior of the sub. There wasn't even a porthole to look out of. In fact, it was rather like standing in one end of a tin can. And, as Tripe after Tripe boarded the submarine, it was difficult to see how all twenty-nine would fit. Mandy worried that they might be breaking some health-and-safety regulation.

She squeezed through the rising throng of cousins and made her way up to the plum-suited woman. 'Excuse me,' she began.

'Yes, my darling, what is it, what can I do for you?' The woman did not look at Mandy as she spoke, but continued to shepherd each new Tripe into the sub. She was unlike any person Mandy had ever met before, and very different to the kinds of people that tended to volunteer with the girl scouts.

'Ah, could you tell me a little more about where we're going?' she asked.

The woman turned her large eyes on Mandy. 'So busy, darling, so busy, preparing for departure.' She smiled brightly. 'Won't you be a love and go and wait with the others? Thank you so much!'

This brief conversation did nothing to remove Mandy's nervousness. As she returned to her cousins, the two mystery buffs, Aurelia and Hortense, greeted her with weak smiles.

'Bit of a tight squeeze, isn't it, Mandy?' said Hortense, looking about anxiously.

The three farm boys, Harry, Larry and Xanthipides, had been so excited at the idea of travelling in a real live submarine that they had been beside themselves from the moment Mandy had announced what she had won. They had been second in the queue – behind Mandy, of course – to clomp down the steel gangway into the interior of the sub and immediately began darting about, poking at things. But when they began to approach the large object that sat at the centre of the sub, which was covered with a white sheet, the woman clapped her hands together and ushered them hastily to the back of the vessel, where they remained, arms folded, looking glum.

Last to come was Little Molly, who bravely refused all offers of help but gingerly picked her way down the steep steps on her own, balancing her large multi-coloured cast precariously on each step.

Ms Follicle clapped her hands together in delight when she saw this. 'Oh, my! How utterly charming!'

As soon as Little Molly reached the floor of the sub, Ms Follicle reached up and slammed the hatch closed with a clang that was so loud, everyone jumped. She then held out her arms. 'You are all very welcome, darlings!' she called. 'I am so delighted to have you all here today aboard my wonderful submarine, *Pride of the Blunt*. I do so hope you will enjoy the wonderful pleasure cruise I have planned! Now, my darlings, we shall be moving from our mooring in a minute or two, so I would ask that, for safety reasons, you all move behind the red line!'

The Tripe children looked about them and saw that by standing behind the red line, the squeeze, which was already quite tight, would be even tighter. Being good, obedient children, however, and not wishing to let Mandy down on her big day, they all began shuffling into the restricted space at the back of the submarine.

'Not you, dear,' said Ms Follicle, laying her hand lightly on Little Molly's shoulder. 'You stay with me.'

There were a few half-smothered *ouch*es and *watch out*s, as toes were trodden on and smaller cousins were accidentally elbowed in the face, but in a matter of a few minutes, the cousins stood, as directed, behind the red line.

Mandy could not now escape the feeling that something wasn't quite right. 'Where are we going, exactly?' she called.

'That's a very good question, darling, thank you so much for asking it!' Ms Follicle beamed. 'Now, if you will all keep still …' She raised her hand, extended a long delicate finger, topped with a long plum-coloured fingernail, and pressed a red button in the wall of the submarine. A barred steel gate shot across the red line, imprisoning Mandy, Oswald and twenty-six of their cousins in one end of the sub.

So it was that Mandy Tripe began to suspect that the letter she had received that morning was not genuine and that she might not, in fact, have won the bike after all.

Polly Mole was sitting at her computer when there was a tap on the window. She turned and saw a slight boy with grey hair squatting outside on the windowsill.

Polly was, of course, unaware of all that had happened to her friend since the liberation of Oswald Tripe earlier that day. When she opened the window, Indigo almost fell into Polly's brown room.

'The Tripes, Polly – Peaches is going to take them all out, every last one. We've got to find them.'

'Oh,' said Polly.

'They're not at home. I just checked. And I need a spare earpiece. You got one?'

'Yes.' Polly calmly went to a drawer in her desk and retrieved a small brown earpiece, which she gave to Indigo, who was still clutching his side. 'You are injured, Indigo.'

'It's nothing. You stay here, Polly. We'll keep in touch. I've got to find them.'

Polly said nothing but stared hard at her friend.

'What, Polly, what is it?'

Polly blinked rapidly. 'I think I know an important fact.'

'Yes?'

'Mandy Tripe thinks she has won the bike offered by the girl scouts for selling the most calendars. And now she is taking part in a novelty trip down the River Blunt with all of her cousins and her brother Oswald.'

'A novelty trip? What kind of novelty trip?'

'In a submarine,' said Polly.

19

The Unfortunate Fate of Little Molly Tripe

Five minutes later, Indigo was driving at full speed across the Eelfields. A submarine. For half a minute he had struggled to remember why a submarine on the River Blunt should sound so familiar. Then it had come to him. A news story, several years old. Something about a strange woman who had held people captive in her submarine. A wig-maker. What was her name? Quisk. Elizabeth. No, Elsbeth. Elsbeth Quisk.

That one little recollection acted like a magnet on a selection of other pieces of information that had been filed away in separate parts of Indigo's brain. The little package in Root's hand as she and Berry went striding off over the bridge that morning, the faint voices that emerged from the smog, the bald spot on Oswald Tripe's head.

Indigo squinted over the steering wheel and through the smog – which seemed even thicker down here by the river – and spotted the grey bulk of the submarine rising above the dark water. He had arrived on the scene not long after the last Tripe had descended into the body of the sleek steel vessel. The van skidded to a halt a few centimetres from the concrete lip of the bank. Indigo threw open the door, leaped from the driver's seat and flung himself on top of the submarine.

'Open this door!' He hammered on the hatch with his fists. 'Open it!'

The door did not open. In fact, there was no response of any kind. Indigo felt as if he was banging on a lump of solid metal. All at once, the sub began to move out and away from the river wall. Indigo quickly scanned the parts that remained above the water. There was no sign of any other way down into it. Realising that he had to take another approach, he leaped back onto dry land before the sub moved too far from the edge of the bank.

'Elsbeth Catherine Quisk' – Polly's voice came over the earpiece – 'has won over twenty-four international awards for her wigs and hairpieces, including the Golden Moustache and the Henri Quiff Memorial Award for Most Outrageous Hairstyle, as well as three Wiggie awards at the Annual Hairpiece Symposium in Butte, Montana. She was also Blunt Person of the Year two years running.'

Indigo pulled open the passenger door of the van, opened the glove compartment and rummaged about. There was nothing there that he could use. A sort of tool box sat between the two seats. Indigo ripped open the cover and found a rope. 'Go on.'

'Six years ago, on 16 October, a highly distressed young man, who was bald, arrived at Blunt Police Station and claimed that he had been imprisoned by Quisk in her submarine, *Pride of the Blunt*. A subsequent police investigation revealed that Quisk had kidnapped an entire secretarial school – the Blunt Secretarial Academy. She kept them locked up in the submarine and shaved their hair periodically for use in her award-winning wigs. She was arrested, but escaped while awaiting trial and subsequently made off in *Pride of the Blunt*. It was thought that she sailed down the Blunt to the open sea. She has not been seen since.'

'Well, Peaches managed to find her,' said Indigo, tying one end of the rope to the back of the van. 'It's their hair, Polly, the Tripes' hair. Peaches sold them to Quisk for their hair. That's why Oswald had a bald patch. Root was bringing her a sample this morning – that's what I saw, that's what sealed the deal. If that sub makes it to the open sea, Polly, those Tripe kids will never be seen again.'

By now the submarine had moved so far from the riverbank that Indigo could no longer have jumped out to it. Instead, he fashioned a loop at the other end of the rope and flung it out, trying to catch the steel mooring post that extended from the top. He missed on his first try, and his second; the rope slid helplessly down the side of the submarine and splashed into the river. But on the third go, it caught, and as the vessel began to drop slowly into the murky waters of the Blunt, Indigo watched the loop tighten about the mooring post.

* * *

The submarine was in uproar. The twenty-eight Tripes imprisoned behind the steel gate were howling and wailing, while also banging the sides of the submarine and the bars of their prison with their fists. Little Molly, who had remained with Elsbeth Quisk outside the steel gate, was scowling her deepest scowl and was ineffectually poking the woman with her crutch.

'Release my cousins, you horrible meanie!'

Quisk, sitting at the controls, flicked at a series of switches, hit the autopilot button, then sighed and stood up.

'Please, darlings,' she called, 'one can hardly hear oneself think!'

The noise did not abate, so she turned to the large, mysterious something which sat at the centre of the sub – the thing the triplets had tried to investigate earlier – and pulled the white sheet from it.

The submarine fell suddenly silent.

It was a little like a dentist's chair, except that dentist's chairs do not have spring-loaded steel restraints attached to the arm- and leg-rests. Nor do they include a specially moulded plastic frame, clearly designed for clamping the head in position. And just above the plastic frame, a set of six robotic arms hung poised, each one terminating in either a blade, a scissors or a pair of needle-nosed pliers.

'This, my dears,' Quisk called, holding her arms out to the dreadful contraption, 'I call the Triminator. It's a little something I had some friends in Trinidad put together for me during the year. Isn't it delightful? Can you guess what it does?' She leaned over and patted Little Molly on the head. 'Can you, my dear? No? Well, let's find out, shall we?'

And with that, she plucked Little Molly from the floor and flung her into the chair.

'NOOOOO!' the imprisoned Tripes cried in unison as the spring-loaded steel restraints shot into position and pinned Little Molly's arms and legs. The plastic head-frame closed about her neck like some kind of terrible sea creature.

'HELP!' cried Little Molly, unable to move anything but her fingers and toes.

Moving lazily, Elsbeth Quisk circled the chair. 'The Triminator is a fully automated involuntary de-hairing machine,' she began, 'designed to accommodate almost any body size and almost any hair type. It works by holding the hair donor perfectly still while these specially designed devices –' she indicated the fiendish looking robotic arms '– strip the donor of his or, as in this case, her hair.' She gazed at it in admiration. 'Isn't it a wonder?'

'You can't turn it on!' Mandy called. 'Please don't do this to Little Molly!'

A chorus of things like 'No, please' and 'Not Little Molly!' followed Mandy's appeal.

'Oh, I won't turn it on,' said Quisk. 'I wouldn't dream of it. Didn't you hear me? The Triminator is fully automated! As we speak, the sensors are analysing the topography of this little girl's head. And any second now ...'

The six robotic arms suddenly flexed, as if a bolt of electricity had shot through them. There was a peculiar grinding noise, then a sudden blur of movement as they went to work.

'EEEEEEEEEEEEEEK!'

Little Molly squealed as if six robot arms were systematically removing every hair from her head. Though she jerked and wriggled and tried to pull away, the restraints held her fast, so that all she could do was squeal, which she did, long and loud.

And then, just as abruptly as it had begun, it ended. The robot arms stopped chopping, whirling and tugging and retreated to their original position, hovering just over the little girl's head, a head that had now been utterly transformed. Seconds earlier, a thick crop of lustrous curls had hung from it. Now, Little Molly's bald head shone like a full moon. Even her eyebrows were gone. Her scalp was dotted with nicks and cuts, but not a single hair remained.

The metal restraints popped open, but Little Molly just lay there, too shocked to move.

'Oh, poor Little Molly!' Mandy shouted.

'You're a monster!' someone else shouted.

And now the submarine was filled with a chorus of remonstrating Tripes, calling out messages of support for Little Molly and berating Elsbeth Quisk for being such a nasty person.

Quisk herself had been watching Little Molly's de-hairing with a fixed smile on her face. Now she moved to the chair and detached a yellow plastic box which sat just beneath the little girl's head. It was full of hair.

She took the box and sailed up to the bars of the prison. 'You think you know how to wear hair?' she cried, taking a fistful from the box and waving it at them. 'You think you know how to wear hair? You don't know how to wear hair! It's wasted on you! Wasted, darlings! Only I, the great Elsbeth Quisk, know how hair should be worn. *You* don't deserve such marvellous hair with your boring short-back-and-sides and your nasty fringes! Hah! I shall bring curly hair back into fashion! Soon you will all become familiar with the Triminator. Over the months and years we will be together, you will –' She stopped suddenly and looked around. 'We're not moving,' she said.

Dropping the box of hair, she went to the periscope, which hung from the ceiling of the sub. Seizing its handles, she spun it round and quickly saw that her submarine was locked into a tug of war with a battered black and amber van which bore the words 'Blunt Home for Nasty Little Liars' on its side.

Up on the riverbank, there was a terrible grinding noise as the two engines – the submarine's and the van's – fought each other. The wheels of the van began to spin, throwing up clods of dirt and sending them raining out onto the water. Indigo pressed his foot further down on the accelerator; the engine roared, but the wheels only spun faster. The van did not move forward. But then, slowly, very slowly, the submarine stopped churning through the water. It remained momentarily immobile. Then it began to move backwards.

'I've got it, Polly,' Indigo panted. 'They're not going anywhere.'

The van began to grind away from the river, dragging the sub with it.

But glancing in the rear-view mirror, Indigo saw the hatch suddenly pop open, and a woman with silvery grey hair piled high on her head and wearing a plum-coloured suit rose up out of the sub. She looked from the van to the rope with a bored expression, then produced a large pair of scissors.

'No!' Indigo shouted.

The woman looked up, smiled coldly and waved a royal wave. She then snipped the rope, which whipped away from the submarine and clattered against the back of the van. The van shot forward.

By the time Indigo managed to stop and get out, the woman had disappeared. All he could see was the top of the submarine sinking rapidly into the murky waters of the Blunt.

20

The Very Dangerous Sisters of Indigo McCloud

In order to reach the open sea, the submarine would have to follow the course of the Blunt right around the edge of the Eelfields, before passing under the bridge by the Crappy Tower. From there, the river left the town, widened and flowed slowly to the sea.

Indigo gunned the engine of the van, which shuddered once, then took off towards the bridge. Glancing out the side window, he could no longer see the submarine and could only guess at its progress. Because of the meandering course of the river, he could easily make it to the bridge before the sub. But what on earth would he do when he got there?

The van skidded to a halt at the Crappy Tower. Indigo jumped out and raced for the bridge. This was old and narrow, with three sets of shallow alcoves running along either side, designed to allow pedestrians to shelter from passing traffic. As he ran, Indigo watched the river closely. This was part of the reason why he did not see the small group of people gathered in the first of the little alcoves on the bridge. As soon as he reached this point, he felt a sudden stab of pain. Something had struck his left shoulder. Before he could even raise a hand or turn to see what had hit him, he felt another blow to his back, then three further blows in rapid succession: to his right knee, his left ankle and his chest. Indigo tried to turn, to get away, and found to his horror that he could not. His body had become completely rigid, as if he had been struck with some kind of freeze ray. Almost as soon as he realised this, he felt himself falling, but he could not even raise his hands to protect his head. He fell, in what felt like slow motion, but just before he crashed to the ground, two pairs of arms seized him roughly.

'Got him!'

'*I* got him!'

'No, you didn't, sludge face!'

'Yes, I did, gobdaw.'

Still bickering, the twins dragged Indigo into the alcove in which they had been hiding and propped him against the wall as if he were a ladder. He could still breathe, he could still move his eyes, but that appeared to be all.

'It's called the mystical five-point paralysis.' The voice was like honey laced with broken glass. 'Su's been dying to try it for ages.'

Peaches stepped from the alcove and struck a pose in the middle of the bridge. She was resplendent in a pink and white polka-dot dress. She wore a pair of outsized sunglasses and her long hair was held in place by a white hair-band.

Beside her, Indigo's littlest sister stood, one leg behind the other, arms raised in a fighting stance. Her jet-black hair framed her twinkling mismatched eyes and evil grin. One word from Peaches and Su would spring into action once more.

'Normally, I would always ensure that I was miles away from one of these little incidents,' Peaches went on, 'but I just couldn't resist this one. The girls and I wanted to be there when every last calendar-selling Tripe was carried out of our lives for ever.'

The horror of being unable to move, unable to speak, made it difficult to take anything else in. Indigo tried to blot out his sisters and focus his attention on his fingers. If he could just get them to move, if he could just coax the tiniest wriggle from them. Time was slipping away. As soon as the sub made it under the bridge, that would be it, they would be gone. There would be no way of getting them back.

Peaches nodded at Su, who stepped forward and, with astonishing speed, struck Indigo five times in the reverse order in which she had hit him before – chest, left ankle, right knee, back and left shoulder. He slumped to the ground. His entire body tingled as if he had been given an electric shock. As Indigo tried to get his breathing under control, as he felt sensation return to his body, his eye fell on a small lump of sandstone that had become dislodged from the bridge and now sat at the base of the alcove in a little pool of sandy dust.

'Go on.' Peaches stood over him. 'Say something like "You won't get away with this, Peaches" or "I'll get you, Peaches".'

Indigo did not really hear her. He stared at the lump of broken sandstone and, as he did, a second invisible lightbulb winked into existence over his head. Indigo had had an idea, a crazy, almost impossible idea, one that would require a host of crazy, almost impossible things to happen in rapid sequence if it was to have any hope of succeeding. The first of these was that the girls would have to let him go.

'No?' said Peaches. 'No threats? Nothing?' She seemed disappointed. She turned and looked back up the bridge. Her face changed and, smiling brightly, she said, 'Oh, look, Indigo, someone to see you!'

Indigo got to his feet and followed Peaches out of the alcove. There was Captain Grotty walking slowly towards him. And when he looked in the other direction, there was Private Winner, making his way from the opposite end of the bridge.

This added a whole new layer of improbability to what was already an almost impossible plan.

Peaches pulled a small mirror from a little pink handbag and inspected her hair. 'Bye bye, brother dear,' she said absently, before replacing the mirror and clicking the bag closed. 'Come, girls, let's watch the show from a safe distance.'

Indigo crouched and collected the chunk of rubble that had fallen from the bridge. As Peaches led his sisters away, he rose to his feet, the little rock cupped in his palm. He had no idea what he might do with it, but it was the closest thing to a weapon he could find. Now, with the odds stacked against him and the chances of success almost nil, Indigo felt a strange kind of freedom. His plan, however improbable, could not possibly make things any worse. And also there was that same sense of rightness. He would fail, yes, but he would fail doing the only thing it made sense to do.

Glancing from Private Winner to Captain Grotty, Indigo spoke rapidly and quietly. 'The Crappy Tower, Polly. No history this time – I need to know about structure. How's it built?'

'OK, Indigo.'

Private Winner, still striding steadily in his direction, flexed his neck so that Indigo could hear it crack. Captain Grotty snapped his teeth together and punched a fist into an open palm.

'Get ready for the pain!' he called. 'Get ready for the pain, you little –'

Not alone did Indigo's crazy, impossible plan require a rapid escape, it also required Captain Grotty and Private Winner's van, which, in the circumstances, they seemed unlikely to offer. A full hand of fingers would also be helpful, together with not bleeding profusely as a result of multiple injuries.

'It's bad luck, you know,' Indigo called to Private Winner, 'walking over the Crappy Bridge front-ways. That's what everyone says round here. You should walk backwards.'

Private Winner wasn't buying it this time. 'I'm gonna pull his head off. You hear me? I'M GONNA PULL YOUR HEAD OFF!' He began to jog along the bridge.

'FIRST I'M GONNA DO HIS FINGERS!' Captain Grotty shouted.

Glancing into the smoky water, Indigo saw a trail of bubbles perhaps thirty metres away and guessed that these marked the progress of the submarine as it sailed beneath the river. There was little time left.

It was Private Winner who stood between Indigo and the van, so there at least he didn't have to make a choice. Trying to ignore the pain in his side, and the pins and needles that still tingled in his fingers and toes, Indigo flexed his shoulders and turned towards the large man, now less than ten metres away.

Polly's voice buzzed in his ear: 'The Crappy Tower and its neighbouring bridge are of sandstone construction. While many forms of sandstone are –'

'Polly, could you just hold that thought for about thirty seconds?'

'Of course, Indigo.'

Private Winner, seeing Indigo turning to face him, adopted a goalkeeper's stance and advanced more slowly, legs splayed, arms outstretched, fingers clawed. 'Oh no you don't,' he said.

Indigo took a deep breath, then took off towards Private Winner at a run. Given how close he was to the exceptionally large man, it was vital that he reach top speed as quickly as possible. Private Winner, scarcely believing that his victim was moving rapidly towards him, stopped dead, crouched even further and got ready to grab.

Because the bridge was so narrow, and Private Winner so big, there was hardly more than seventy centimetres between each of his clawed hands and the wall. But Indigo had no intention of dodging past him. Just as they were about to meet, as Private Winner's shoulders opened up and his great arms were about to close on his quarry, Indigo suddenly produced the stone and flung it at Private Winner's bull-like head. This close, he could not miss. The big man's eyes widened as the little piece of bridge came flying towards his nose; his arms began to move protectively towards his face; and, as they did, Indigo McCloud took flight. Spreading his arms wide, just as he did when he leaped between the roofs of Blunt, Indigo rose through the air and sailed untouched over Private Winner as the stone struck the man's nose and bounced off.

'OWK!' Private Winner cried in pain.

Indigo landed, rolled, rose smoothly to his feet and took off towards the van. 'OK, Polly,' he breathed, 'tell me what you know.'

'The Crappy Tower and its neighbouring bridge are of sandstone construction. While many forms of sandstone are suitable for use as building materials, it is relatively soft. Erosion by the wind has over time given the tower its distinctive misshapen appearance. It has also undermined the integrity of the structure, which is why it is currently condemned, awaiting demolition.'

Indigo had reached the van by now. He dived inside and turned on the ignition. As he did, he glanced up and saw both Captain Grotty and Private Winner racing towards him. 'OK,' he said, 'so the tower's a bit fragile?'

'Yes,' said Polly. 'What are you going to do, Indigo?'

Indigo didn't answer.

He pushed down on both the accelerator and the clutch, so that the engine roared. He could see Captain Grotty's mouth opening and closing as he ran towards the van, but could not hear his threats or rude words over the noise.

Flicking the gear stick into first, Indigo released the clutch, the wheels spun and the back of the van skidded first one way, then the other. Private Winner reached the driver's door and grabbed the handle with both hands. Indigo had, of course, locked the door, but as the van took off, Private Winner clung to it, swinging both legs up to try to wrench it open.

Indigo rolled the window down a crack. 'That's bad luck, you know.'

Private Winner roared with rage and pulled with all his might. The door came flying off its hinges, so that both it and he went flying backwards. The enormous man landed spreadeagled on the grass, struck his head and was knocked out cold.

'Told you,' said Indigo quietly.

'Indigo,' came Polly's voice over the earpiece, 'I strongly recommend that you do not attempt to demolish the tower without specialist equipment and safety gear. My calculations place the risk of death at above 94 per –'

'Thank you, Polly.' Indigo pulled out the earpiece and shoved it into the pocket of his jacket.

And as he did, Indigo McCloud had a sudden recollection. He remembered being flung bodily, many years earlier, into the grass and weeds that grew alongside the motorway. He remembered how his mother had fought to save him. If she hadn't sacrificed herself, he would not be alive today.

He glanced at the speedometer. It had climbed steadily, and now, with less than six or seven metres to the river, it crossed the 150 kph mark and began to nuzzle 160. Gripping the steering wheel, Indigo took careful aim. There was no further time to check the progress of the submarine. He could only hope that his plan would work, that it would not be too late.

Three metres, two metres... As the needle on the speed-ometer hit 162 kph, the van from the Blunt Home for Nasty Little Liars crested the riverbank and shot out over the river. Peaches, Su, Root and Berry watched as it flew through the air, then smashed, with a horrible metallic crunching noise, into the base of the Crappy Tower.

21

The Secret Fear of Peaches McCloud

The Crappy Tower, huge and knobbled and brown, seemed to quiver slightly. Those who witnessed the impact or who looked up when they heard the terrible sound of the crash blinked, thinking they had seen the monstrosity wobble slightly. Perhaps, they thought, it was just an optical illusion, the way a moving cloud can sometimes appear to be still and give the impression that it is the building in the foreground that has moved. Or perhaps it was a trick of the smoke permanently drifting down over Blunt and everything in it.

Next came a sound like an elephant in steel wellingtons dancing on a bag of bones. And then, like a great tree that has just succumbed to the woodcutter's axe, the tower teetered once, then slowly pitched forward and crashed down into the river in a deafening crescendo of water and rock. A huge cloud of sandy-coloured dust rose into the air.

The submarine had been almost beside the tower when it fell. Down at the controls, Elsbeth Catherine Quisk had little time to divert or reverse or kill the engines, and with a terrible grinding of metal and stone, the vessel rose up against the pile of rubble that now stretched across the river, until fully half of it stuck out of the water at an alarming angle. For a moment, it looked as though it might rise completely from the water, but then the terrible grinding faded to a creaking, watery silence, and there the submarine remained, unable to move forward or back.

Indigo's sisters had sheltered from the falling tower in a doorway. As the dust began to settle, Peaches was the first to return to the river railing. She ripped the sunglasses from her face and scanned the rubble, her eyes blazing. 'Where is he?'

The twins and Tsunami joined her. All four squinted through the smoke and dust and water. The river surged about the fallen tower and the beached submarine, but there was no sign of their brother.

Root was the first to speak. 'He's dead, Peaches,' she said slowly.

Berry did not disagree.

The twins and Tsunami turned to look at their big sister, their faces uncertain. Enslaving the twenty-nine Tripe cousins was one thing. Killing your brother was quite another. It was as if they were waiting to be told what to feel.

And then a curious thing happened. A look of disquiet passed across the face of Peaches McCloud.

'Peaches?' said Root.

The moment passed quickly. Peaches's fingers tightened on the guardrail. Her lips curled into a sneer as she stared down at the submarine, sticking up out of the water. 'He saved them,' she spat. 'He saved them.'

By now a crowd had begun to gather by the river as the people of Blunt came to investigate the mighty crash and the sudden disappearance of the Crappy Tower from the skyline. Everyone had hated the tower and was sick to the teeth of people – especially people from Cragmire and Bulstrode – making stupid jokes about the enormous poo that could be seen from almost everywhere in town. Now, all of a sudden, when everyone thought they would have to put up with it for ever, Indigo McCloud had single-handedly wiped it from the map. People surged about the river railings, pointing and laughing and hugging each other.

'Somebody's only gone and flushed it away!' a man cried, to peals of laughter.

The submarine, of course, was a very curious addition to what was otherwise an occasion for celebration. The townspeople pointed and nudged each other and asked if the beached sub could possibly belong to the notorious kidnapper and disgraced wig-maker.

They did not have to wonder long, for all of a sudden, a loud metallic cracking noise rang out across the river. A crack appeared at the back of the submarine and raced along its length. Though the impact of the collision appeared to have left the sub intact, the structure could not survive with one half protruding so far above the water.

With another metallic groan, the submarine, like an overripe pea pod, split open, revealing a host of exceptionally curious things inside. A sharply dressed woman, her grey hair slightly mussed, clung to what appeared to be a rather intimidating looking dentist's chair. There was also a small bald child with crutches and a cast sobbing theatrically, together with a large pile of groaning chestnut-haired children.

Elsbeth Quisk looked up at the crowd of faces staring down at her. 'I'm back, darlings,' she called. 'Did you miss me?'

'It's her!' someone shouted. 'It's Quisk!'

The Tripes, released from their prison by the disintegrating submarine, began to help each other out through the breach in the metal. Someone among the crowd brought a ladder from a nearby factory and lowered it down onto the rubble.

Peaches, meanwhile, regarded the scene in disgust. Her terrible vengeance against the Tripes had come to nothing. With a final snort of fury, she turned from the railing and began to squeeze through the crowd. At this point, however, the press of bodies was too great.

'Su!' she barked, 'get me out of here.'

Su, who stood a little way away, reacted instantly. The littlest McCloud karate-chopped her way through the crowd, her progress marked by a series of *ow*s, *eek*s and squeals as anyone who stood in her way was hacked down or shoved to the side. She picked Peaches up and turned to carry her back.

By now, however, news of Elsbeth Quisk's sudden return to Blunt had rippled through the crowd and, just as Su lifted Peaches off her feet, there was a sudden rush of people. Caught off balance, Su went reeling backwards and her arms, which still contained Peaches, flew up into the air. It was an act of pure reflex, one which she couldn't control, but the consequences of which would haunt her for quite some time to come.

'Aaaaaaagh!' cried Peaches, reaching out and trying to grab something, anything. There was nothing there to grab.

'No!' cried Su. Diving backwards, she tried to reverse what she had done, but it was too late. Tsunami McCloud had inadvertently flung her eldest sister over the river railings.

'Peaches!' Root and Berry called together. The three girls stared in horror at their whirling, roaring, white-legged, polka-dotted sister, but there was nothing any of them could do to save her.

'She's going to drown!' cried Berry.

But there was no splash. Peaches McCloud landed with a clatter and a grunt into the welcoming arms of the Triminator, which had not been damaged in any way by the collision. Before she could react, the steel restraints sprang into place and the plastic head-frame closed about her neck, rendering her completely immobile. Looking up, she found herself staring into the saffron eyes of Elsbeth Quisk. Quisk raised one eyebrow.

'Get me out of here!' said Peaches, her left eyelid quivering.

'Would if I could, darling.' Quisk shrugged. 'All automatic now, you know.'

The six robotic arms suddenly flexed, as if a bolt of electricity had shot through them. There was a peculiar grinding noise, and then a sudden blur of movement as they went to work.

'Nooooooooo!' cried Peaches. 'NOOOOOOOOOO!'

Horrified at what she had caused, Su fought her way back to the railings and, without a thought for her own safety, flung herself over them and landed like a tiny avenging goddess on the floor of the submarine. As the robotic arms continued to shave, pluck and snip at Peaches, Tsunami set to work, chopping at and kicking the monstrous machine. The Triminator was, however, very well made. Su's frenzied violence did nothing to halt its attack.

'GET ME OUT OF HERE!' Peaches roared.

Now Su changed tack, and instead of attacking the machine, she leaped up onto the chair and seized Peaches under her arms. With a mighty roar and a supreme effort, she began to pull her from the chair. Unfortunately for Peaches, that mighty roar and supreme effort coincided exactly with the conclusion of the de-hairing process. The restraints popped open. Su ripped her sister from the chair with such force that, for the second time in as many minutes, Peaches McCloud went whirling through the air. This time, there was a splash.

We all have a secret fear. For Lucy Jones, it was birds; for Mandy Tripe, it was spiders.

For Peaches McCloud, it was eels.

Few, except perhaps her sisters, knew that Peaches was plagued by a recurring nightmare. At least once every week, she would awake covered in cold sweat and breathing rapidly. In her dream, she was always sinking slowly into a mass of writhing yellow eels. As they pulled her down, they would whisper terrible things to her, before attacking her with their strong jaws and rows and rows of small, hard teeth.

As soon as Peaches McCloud landed in the river, the closest eel to her emitted a chemical into the water. This chemical spread rapidly through the river, striking the sensory organs of every eel within half a mile. The chemical signalled one thing: *Lunch is served.*

The waters closed in on the freshly shaved Peaches like an icy blanket. She flailed and splashed and fought her way upwards as, from every part of the river, the vicious yellow eels of the Blunt surged towards her. The first closed its teeth upon her shin. Peaches tried to cry out, but instead took in a mouthful of river water. The second took a bite out of her elbow. The third sank its teeth into her knee. Peaches screamed and choked and kicked as the vicious little monsters came at her from all angles, but it was no use. She was utterly overwhelmed. She shut her eyes as her nightmare came to life and the slimy, twisting bodies of the eels surrounded her.

By the time Su made it to her sister's side and hauled her bodily from the river, Peaches McCloud had been bitten eighty-seven times. As she rose up out of the water, more than forty of the very biggest eels still clung to her, their teeth in her skin and lodged in the folds of her polka-dotted dress. Half-roaring, half-screaming, she batted wildly at the clinging, writhing beasts. 'GET THEM OFF ME! GET THEM OFF ME!'

It is at this point that the sludge barge makes a sudden return to the story. Shortly after it had almost delivered Mandy Tripe to Auntie Maggie's Big Hairy Spider Emporium, the horse which had been towing the barge had finally broken free. As she galloped off down the towpath pursued by her handler, the barge began drifting aimlessly down the Pyewkenocky Canal. Two days later, it crossed the little weir outside Mullet and plunged into the River Blunt. Still half-full of sludge, it was carried slowly towards the town of Blunt, where it arrived at 4:17 p.m. on the day in question. With all eyes on the fallen tower and the beached submarine, few people noticed its acceleration towards the scene of the incident

'Get them off me! GET THEM OFF ME!'

The panicked girls joined Su in trying to pull the eels away but they were large and muscular and very slippery. Peaches danced about on the rubble, her bald head shining like a highly polished ostrich egg. Coughing up mouthfuls of murky river water, she flapped and screamed and batted blindly at the writhing eels.

All four girls were so intent on this work that they knew nothing about the sludge barge until it crashed headlong into the fallen tower. The remaining sludge – approximately 12.8 metric tonnes – surged forward in a great grey–black wave. Root, Berry and Su looked up in horror as the sludge crested the stern of the barge, blotting out the sun, then came crashing down upon them in a foul-smelling avalanche of filth.

Up on the bridge and along the river railings, the twenty-nine liberated Tripes, along with hundreds of townspeople, watched the wave of sludge flow like treacle from the rubble into the river, filling up the abandoned submarine and burbling thickly over the side. One by one, the McCloud girls rose up out of the filth, wailing and coughing and stumbling about, trying to scrape the awful stuff from eyes, mouths and hair. The attacking eels, clearly as unhappy as the girls with recent events, wriggled back over the sludgy rubble, plopped into the sludgy water and sped off and away from the scene of the catastrophe.

22

The Triumph of
Chief Inspector Milkweed

Despite Root's pronouncement, Indigo McCloud was not quite dead. Just before the van struck the base of the tower, he had leaped from the driver's side, which, thanks to Private Winner's exertions, now lacked a door, and been catapulted out and away from the river.

When one is travelling freely through the air at 148 kph, it is very difficult to control how one lands. Indigo's flight took him past the tower, over the narrow road behind it and into the yard of the disused toothbrush-holder factory beyond. Indigo skidded to a halt in a patch of weeds and tall yellowing grass strewn with tin cans, old shopping bags and assorted rubbish. He lay there breathlessly beneath the factory's rusted fire escape as the tower pitched forward into the river.

He heard the crash, looked up to see the dust cloud rise into the air and knew at least that the tower had fallen. He could not be sure, however, that his desperate plan had halted the submarine. Groaning, he turned over and slowly got to his feet.

It was at this point that Indigo heard the dogs.

In all that had happened since the morning, he had completely forgotten about them, but now, once again, he heard the sound of barking from somewhere nearby and recognised it instantly. The police, he realised, must have been circling the town for hours, trying to find him again. And now they had.

He had to get away, and fast.

But before Indigo could act on this instinct, a shadow fell across him, wiry arms spun him around and he was once more confronted by the glinting eyes, greasy black hair and minty fresh breath of Captain Grotty.

'You're gonna pay for that van, kid,' he said through gritted teeth, 'in blood and bone.'

Indigo tried to pull himself away, but Captain Grotty seized him by the lapels and held him tight. Bruised and battered by his encounters with the two psychopaths, not to mention Tsunami and, of course, his death-defying leap from the doomed van, Indigo had very little energy left.

'I'm gonna start with your nose.'

Captain Grotty opened his mouth wide and closed in on Indigo's face.

Then the dogs barked again, much closer this time, and for the third time that day, a lightbulb sparked to life just above the grey head of Indigo McCloud.

'They're looking for you, you know,' he panted, stretching his neck away from Captain Grotty's bared teeth. 'You think I didn't report you? The cops are out there looking for two guys in army clothes.'

'Shaddup!' said Captain Grotty,

'Hear those dogs? That's the cops. Two guys in military fatigues, that's who they're looking for. You're as good as caught.'

Indecision rippled across Captain Grotty's face. He cast a brief glance over his shoulder. The crowd, full of bobbing heads and obvious good cheer, was swelling thickly about the riverside. Were those high visibility vests that could be seen among them the cops?

'Gimme your jacket!' Captain Grotty pinned Indigo against the wall of the factory with one hand and wriggled out of his army jacket.

'What?' said Indigo, trying to appear dismayed.

'I said, gimme your jacket!'

Captain Grotty spun Indigo round and ripped the jacket from his shoulders.

That was all Indigo needed. As soon as Captain Grotty's hands closed upon the torn aviator jacket, he wrenched himself free.

'GET BACK …'

But it was too late. With his last reserves of energy, Indigo launched himself upwards and grabbed at the base of the toothbrush-holder factory's fire escape. As Captain Grotty lunged after him, Indigo swung upwards. He felt the clawed fingers of Captain Grotty's hand graze his leg.

The man roared. 'I'LL KILL YOU.'

But Indigo had landed on the first of the fire-escape's platforms and Captain Grotty could do little but shake his fist and dance with pop-eyed rage in the weeds and rubbish below. Knowing that the dogs were almost upon him, Indigo wasted no time. Within seconds he was halfway up the side of the building.

He was free, and he knew he was free and that knowledge fuelled his rapid ascent. This was home ground; this was the secret, empty world above the town that he and he alone owned. This was where Indigo McCloud became the truest version of himself. He threw not a single glance behind him as he climbed and climbed and climbed.

Two large German shepherds, barking madly and straining at their leashes, burst through the crowd, followed closely by their two handlers and the red-faced, purple-nosed, small-eyed, bespectacled bulk of Chief Inspector Milkweed. Milkweed was so intent on capturing the Breadcrumb Bandit that he barely noticed the gathering crowd or the fallen tower or the beached submarine in the river. He had spent the day, just as Indigo had supposed, circling the town with the dogs, refusing to give up the chase.

One of his junior officers tapped him on the shoulder. 'Sir, it would appear that a submarine has –'

The chief inspector, his eyes like tiny specks of coal, waved the man away irritably. 'Never mind that! The dogs have the scent! We nearly have him. Focus, Officer, focus!'

As they carved a path through the crowd, no-one, not even the dogs, noticed the small figure cresting the top of the toothbrush-holder factory and disappearing from view, but everyone saw the small man with the greasy black hair wearing the torn aviator jacket and leaning nonchalantly against the wall, whistling 'Mary Had a Little Lamb' and trying to appear innocent.

At the scent of the aviator jacket, the dogs went wild. Three more policemen emerged from the crowd and stood staring at the small man, whose whistled tune slowly died.

He smiled weakly, then turned and ran.

In less than a minute, Captain Grotty had been expertly brought down by a rugby tackle from one of the policemen. He was handcuffed, hauled to his feet and presented to Chief Inspector Milkweed, who stared down at him through his thick spectacles.

'So, Breadcrumb Bandit,' he boomed, 'we meet again!'

'What?' said Captain Grotty.

'Ah, yes,' Chief Inspector Milkweed went on. 'You have wreaked havoc in my town for long enough! But crime never pays, Breadcrumb Bandit! You will swiftly learn that you do not trifle with the forces of the law! Most particularly, you do not trifle with Chief Inspector Linus K. Milkweed.' Milkweed nodded at the policemen. 'Take him away, boys.'

23

The Peculiar Feeling
of Indigo McCloud

It was two days later.

Dusk.

The twin red and black chimney stacks of the Christmas-tree factory pushed their endless streams of grey–black smoke up through the drizzle; the citizens of Blunt turned up their collars and moved more quickly along the cobbles. Down at the Eelfields, the clean-up operation was in full swing. A construction crew was busy retrieving masonry from the river, while a team of engineers directed the operation. A very large crane had been set up alongside and was slowly winching the wreck of the sludge-filled submarine from the water.

Up in the donkey sanctuary, a donkey called Alan looked up into the smoky grey sky and felt the rain fall on his grizzled donkey features. For no reason other than that he was a donkey, and this is what donkeys do, he threw back his head and began hee-hawing loudly. His fellow donkeys joined in the chorus as, down in the accordion factory, the testers started into a new batch and began playing the scale of B-flat minor over and over again.

Down in the cells beneath Blunt Police Station, Captain Grotty lay on his narrow bunk and clamped a pillow over his head to try to drown out the music. On the opposite bunk, Private Winner peered at the newspaper he had found. It was several months old. He was reading, or trying to read, the horoscopes.

'Oooh, listen to this, Ern. "You will be taking a long journey and staying away for ... for a prolonged period of time." Hear that, Ern? Well, it's just right, innit? I mean, if you get done for all that stuff they said you done, in the breadcrumb factory and that –'

Captain Grotty swung the pillow at him. 'Shaddup!'

A little further down the corridor, Elsbeth Catherine Quisk called from her bunk. 'A little quiet, darlings, please. One can scarcely hear oneself think!' She was fiddling with a hairpin. She had taken the clips, bobbles and assorted accessories from her hair, so that it was no longer piled upon her head but fell smoothly down her back.

Captain Grotty sat up and shouted, 'You shut up! If it wasn't for your stupid submarine, I wouldn't be here, would I?'

Quisk shook her head and tutted. 'Self-pity is so last year, darling. Why don't you consider a new hobby? Sky-diving, perhaps, preferably without a parachute.'

Standing up, Quisk moved to the door of her cell and inserted one end of the hairpin, which she had twisted into a peculiar shape, into the lock. Within seconds, there was a click. She silently opened the door and let herself out. Private Winner, intent on his paper, and Captain Grotty, his head back under the pillow, never saw her move quietly up the stairs.

Not far away, in his office in the same building, Chief Inspector Linus Kelvin Milkweed was on the phone.

'Yes, of course, Commissioner, she's in the cells underneath the station as I speak. ... Oh no, sir! There is no way she could escape again, sir, certainly not, sir! ... Why, yes, sir, I would be honoured if you would visit ... Tomorrow morning? Excellent, sir, I look forward to it! Thank you, sir. Good evening, sir!'

Milkweed, his small red features glowing with delight, lowered the phone, sat back in his chair and smiled the broadest smile that he had ever smiled.

'The commissioner himself,' he said, 'coming to my town! To see me! To applaud me on some excellent police work!'

He leaned forward and hit the button on the intercom. 'Ferguson? Are there any of those cake pops left? Ferguson?'

When Ferguson failed to respond, Milkweed, muttering irately, stood up and went out into the lobby. The man did not appear to be behind his desk, but a scuffling sound and a muted groan made Milkweed bend down to peer beneath it. There lay Ferguson, his hands, arms and legs trussed up with an assortment of elasticated hair bobbles, rendering him completely immobile. A hairnet stuffed into his mouth was held in place with a hair-band. There was a large, nasty-looking bump on his forehead.

'Ferguson!' said Milkweed, staring at him. 'What on earth?' He bent down and pulled the hairnet from his subordinate's mouth.

'It's Quisk, sir,' panted Ferguson. 'I … I think she got out, sir.'

'WHAT?'

Milkweed turned and dashed downstairs to the cells. The door of Elsbeth Quisk's cell stood open. It was, of course, completely empty.

'Ho ho, copper!' Captain Grotty taunted him. 'She's flown the coop!'

'No!' cried Milkweed, spinning around and leaping back up the stairs as fast as his large frame could carry him. He dashed through the lobby and tore open the front door. It was starting to get dark. The narrow cobbled street was empty. Rain fell softly through the smoke.

Milkweed fell to his knees on the footpath. 'No!' he cried. 'NOOOOOOOOOO!'

Meanwhile, in another part of town, Elsbeth Quisk made her way silently through the dusky streets in Officer Ferguson's overcoat, a large yellow container of blond hair concealed beneath it. Just as she turned onto a grimy street, a truck pulled up alongside her and a man in a cap leaned out of the cab.

''Scuse me, missus?'

'Yes?' said Quisk.

'Lookin' for Adenoid Terrace.'

'Is that so?' Quisk eyed the man and his truck carefully. 'You know it?'

'May I ask who it is you are looking for?'

'Hang on.' The man disappeared into his cab again and Quisk heard the rustle of paper. He reappeared. 'Special delivery for Peaches McCloud. Lovely new bike. Says here that she won it in some sort of competition.'

Mandy and the other Tripes had been so busy looking for Oswald that they'd failed to sell a single calendar since the girl scouts meeting. Su, Root and Berry however, had redoubled their efforts and, in the end, the McCloud girls outsold Mandy by a single calendar.

Elsbeth Quisk smiled broadly. 'What joy!' she said. 'I am she!'

'Oh, yeah? That's lucky!'

'I will take it now, thank you very much.'

Three minutes later, she was bicycling unsteadily down the road atop a brand-new pink and white bicycle, a large container of blond hair strapped to the carrier, Ferguson's coat flapping in the breeze. It had been many years since Quisk had been on a bicycle, and not far from Adenoid Terrace, she almost collided with a young girl walking in the opposite direction.

'Watch out!' said the girl, who looked a little pale in the streetlight – as if she had not been out of the house in a while. She fixed Quisk with a pair of penetrating blue eyes.

'A thousand apologies, darling!' Quisk wrinkled her nose at the girl's spiky hair and sped off down the street.

Lucy Jones looked nervously at the sky. The rain continued to fall steadily but there were no birds to be seen. Then, from somewhere down over the river, she heard a seagull shriek. Lucy tensed, fighting the urge to scream and run.

'I can do this,' she said quietly to herself. 'I can do this.' She continued on her way, returning to her own house at

Number 37, Adenoid Terrace ten minutes later, where her parents met her at the door.

'Well done, Lucy!' said her mother, giving her a hug.

'You did it!' said her father.

Up in her room, Polly stood at the window and watched the Jones parents congratulate their daughter. She picked up the radio and spoke into it. 'Lucy Jones has just arrived safely back to her house, Indigo.'

Perched on the roof of the Christmas-tree factory, Indigo McCloud breathed out slowly. 'Good.'

He stood up and smelled the smoke in the air. It continued to spew out into the twilight overhead. He could see the grey outline of the town with its collection of streets, houses and assorted industrial buildings, most of which were empty and crumbling. Through the smoky evening air, he heard the strains of the accordions mingling with the braying of the donkeys. He could see the floodlights down by the river, where the men still worked, clearing away the fallen tower and mangled submarine.

Indigo had found his father the previous day in the fourth-storey waiting room of the hospital on Pox Street, where the girls had been brought following their ordeal. The younger three were not badly hurt. All were suffering from mild sludge poisoning and each had to be hosed down over a dozen times to try to rid them of the smell of the stuff.

Peaches, however, was still haunted by the eel attack. She could not doze off for more than a few seconds before the nightmares resumed. She sat propped up in bed, bald head shining like a newly polished bowling ball, her eyes red from lack of sleep. Every so often she would twitch and shriek and flap at the imaginary eel she thought she could feel squirming up through the sheets.

When Indigo entered the waiting room, the TV on the wall showed pictures of Captain Grotty and Private Winner. The newsreader was saying that they were suspected of a long list of crimes in the Bulstrode area and that the police had been looking for them for months.

'Oh, Indigo, you're safe!' Tim McCloud threw his arms around his son. 'Can you believe it? Those two weren't the genuine article at all! They were criminals of some sort, and they totally fooled poor Peaches. Have you seen her?' Tim's eyes began to tear up and he wrung his hands. 'Oh, Indigo, she's a wreck! You don't blame her, do you? You don't really think she's evil, do you?'

Through the glass in the door, Indigo saw his eldest sister sitting up in bed, and did a double take. With neither blond tresses nor carefully shaped eyebrows – without eyebrows of any sort – she was barely recognisable.

'Evil?' said Indigo. He nodded at the TV screen. 'Well, that would explain why she set those two on me, wouldn't it?'

Tim stared at his son, his expression uncertain.

Indigo smiled. 'Only kidding, Dad. Peaches is one in a million, I know that.'

'Oh, Indigo!' Tim turned to look at his golden princess. 'Why do bad things happen to good people? What a terribly unjust world we live in!'

* * *

Back on the roof of the Christmas-tree factory, Indigo heard a seagull shriek and saw it swoop low over the broken cobbles and patchwork roofs of Adenoid Terrace.

'It's possible to get over something then, don't you think, Polly?'

'Get over something. You do not mean a physical obstacle, do you?'

'Lucy. Something horrible happened to her, but she got over it.'

Polly didn't respond.

'I mean, it didn't *unhappen*, did it? She was attacked by those birds. It still happened, but she got over ... no, she's getting over it. She'll be OK.'

'Yes, Indigo.'

'It's possible to get over things.' Indigo's mind drifted back now to the grass and weeds by the edge of the motorway. He heard the surge of the truck's engine, then the deafening crash of the tumbling toilets. 'She'll always remember that, being attacked, being terrified, right? But that's OK. It's OK to remember it ... you just can't let it ... tell you what to do, right?'

There was silence on the other end.

'That's it, really, isn't it, Polly? You can't let it tell you what to do.'

Then Polly said, 'Ducks.'

'What?'

'I can talk about ducks, when you remember.'

Indigo nodded to himself in the darkness. 'Yeah, ducks.'

'Would you like me to talk about ducks now?'

'That would be nice, Polly.'

Polly cleared her throat. 'While it is widely known that swans have one partner with whom they mate for life, few people are aware that the paradise shelduck native to New Zealand is also monogamous. In fact, according to folklore …'

Indigo turned his gaze towards the huge, rambling hospital on Pox St and stared at the fourth-floor window of the room where his sister twitched and slept. And as he stared, Indigo McCloud experienced a peculiar feeling, one which took him a little time to identify. It was not contentment, and certainly not happiness. A certain sense of accomplishment? No. As he gazed into the darkened windows of the hospital, Indigo realised that the peculiar feeling wasn't actually a feeling at all. It was the absence of a feeling.

Fear.

Indigo McCloud was not afraid.

Acknowledgements

Big thanks to Brian Finnegan, who helped get the idea off the ground in the first place, and who provided great advice and encouragement through the early drafts.

Thank you also to my family for all their love, inspiration and fun.

This does not mean, however, that any of you are getting your hands on my royalties.

We hope you have enjoyed reading *The Very Dangerous Sisters of Indigo McCloud*. On the following pages you will find out about some other Little Island books you might like to read.

Little Island

THE FREE RANGE DETECTIVE AGENCY
By Jed Lynch
Illustrated by Stephen Stone

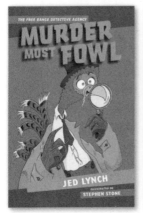 

Seamus the private investigator is no chicken. He's a turkey.

He may not be the best detective in town. In fact, he may be the worst. But with a bit of luck and some help from his friends (a meerkat and a mole) he will somehow crack the case.

'I laughed so much I laid an egg. GENIUS.'
– Dustin the Turkey

HOW TO BAKE A SAUSAGE DOG

By Kirsten Reinhardt

Illustrated by David Roberts

Translated from German by Siobhán Parkinson

Eleven-year-old Fennymore lives with his strange great-aunt (who eats sausage dogs) in an old house with only a magical bike (that thinks it's a horse) for company.

After his great-aunt dies, Fennymore sets off with his new friend Fizzy (who lives in a supermaket) to find his parents, who mysteriously disappeared. They fall foul of a silvery grey gentleman and an evil doctor who wants to get his hands on Fennymore's father's secret invention.

'Eccentricity and zaniness abound, with more than a suggestion of the sinister ... this novel sparkles with wit and inventiveness.'
– *The Irish Times*

'a fast-paced adventure story. Exquisite black-and-white line drawings by David Roberts make it especially pleasing.' – *The Irish Independent*

About the Author

John Hearne was born in Wexford in 1970. He worked as an economist in Dublin before changing direction and becoming a freelance writer. He has ghostwritten and edited a range of best-selling books, while his journalism has appeared in numerous national and international newspapers and magazines. He was also shortlisted for the Hennessy New Irish Writing Awards. He lives in Galway with Marie and their four children.

About Little Island

Founded in 2010 in Dublin, Ireland, Little Island Books publishes good books for young minds, from toddlers all the way up to older teens. In 2019 Little Island won a Small Press of the Year award at the British Book Awards. As well as publishing a lot of new Irish writers and illustrators, Little Island publishes books in translation from around the world.

www.littleisland.ie